nowhere,
now here

Also by Ann Howard Creel
A Ceiling of Stars

More AG Fiction for Older Girls
★
Smoke Screen
by Amy Goldman Koss
★
The Secret Voice of
Gina Zhang
by Dori Jones Yang
★
A Song for Jeffrey
by Constance M. Foland
★
Going for Great
by Carolee Brockmann

nowhere,
now here

Ann Howard Creel

Published by Pleasant Company Publications
Text © Copyright 2000 by Ann Howard Creel
Cover Illustration © Copyright 2000 by Chris Kasch

Visit our Web site at **www.americangirl.com**

Printed in the United States of America.
First Edition
00 01 02 03 04 05 06 RRD 10 9 8 7 6 5 4 3 2 1

The characters and events portrayed in this book are fictitious.
Any similarity to real persons, living or dead, is coincidental
and not intended by the author.

American Girl® and AG Fiction™ are trademarks of Pleasant Company.

Editorial Development: Andrea Weiss
Art Direction and Design: Joshua Mjaanes, Ingrid Slamer
Alpaca Consultants: Dr. Judy Batker and Country View Veterinary Service
of Oregon, Wisconsin; Karla Ditsch-Moen, Alpaca Breeder

Library of Congress Cataloging-in-Publication Data
Creel, Ann Howard.
Nowhere, now here / Ann Howard Creel.—1st ed.
p. cm.   "AG fiction."
Summary: When her family moves from Florida to the Colorado prairie to
raise alpacas, twelve-year-old Laney must leave behind the ocean she loves
and accept the new landscape and life ahead of her.
ISBN 1-58485-199-6 (pbk)   ISBN 1-58485-200-3 (hc)
[1. Moving, Household—Fiction. 2. Prairies—Fiction. 3. Alpaca—Fiction.
4. Ranch life—Fiction.] I. Title.
PZ7.C8625 No 2000   [Fic]—dc21   99-086219

To my favorite American girls,
Barbi and Jamie

contents

curves in the road

I've always loved curves in the road,
especially the blind ones—the ones
that are so sharp you can't even
see around them. When I was
little, too little to ride in the
front seat, I remember
clinging to the vinyl-covered
armrest of our old Subaru
wagon, giggling and
squealing as my dad veered
around the winding roads
of the Florida Everglades. But
three months ago, life threw me
a curve bigger than any I had ever
imagined. And this time I wasn't laughing.

[1]

leaving

I knew something was up as soon as my sister Angela and I arrived home from school. I felt it the minute I walked in the front door. Mom was home early from work. I had seen her car in the driveway. And from the kitchen came the sound of spoons against pans and the smell of food cooking—and my mom never cooked. I could only remember her making dinner twice in the past year, and one of those times was Thanksgiving.

I followed the smells into the kitchen, and there was Mom wearing a chef's apron someone had given her years before. Someone who didn't know her very well at all.

"What's going on?" I asked.

Mom was busy whisking something in a bowl. She lifted her eyes just for a second, long enough for me to be startled by what I saw. In my entire twelve-year life span, I don't think I've ever seen my mom's face look so great. Her skin had this bright kind of glow, shimmery like seashells at sunset.

She said, "I'm trying your grandmother's pot roast recipe. We're going to start eating real food for a change."

I slung my backpack up on the counter. "Why?"

"Oh, Dad and I have some very exciting news, but you'll have to wait until dinner." She kept on whisking. "We want to tell you when we can all sit down together."

Angela strolled into the kitchen and gave Mom a soft smack on the cheek. Then she grabbed some pot holders and stood by the stove to assist. Typical Angela, my oh-so-perfect sister. For years, I had held out hope that as soon as she hit thirteen, she would change. I had always heard about kids turning into monsters or something when they become teenagers. But not my sister. She was more perfect than ever.

Angela kept glancing up and sharing little smiles with Mom, the kind you share when you know something someone else doesn't.

"Hand me that slotted spoon," Mom said to Angela.

Angela peeked into a saucepan. "This looks great."

They were just so comfortable, too chummy for words. And that's when I guessed it—Angela was already in on this huge piece of news. Really it shouldn't have come as a surprise. Angela was always getting special treatment, not just because she was the older one, but because she was so "mature" and "responsible."

I went up to my room and began pacing the floor. I had one of those seriously jumpy feelings in my stomach. For months my mom and dad, who used to be pretty acceptable parents, had been having big discussions about our lives. Dad had been complaining about his job, whining about having to commute to the city, and telling us all about the way "It Used to Be" when he was a kid.

My dad grew up in the country, in some dumpy little town surrounded by ranches and farms. Dad's best friend lived on one of the ranches, a place that Dad described as if it were paradise. He talked about it every time he'd had a bad day at work, or whenever he could make somebody listen. Angela, Mom, and I had been listening to "It Used to Be" stories for as long as I could remember.

But lately his stories had turned into an almost constant blast from the past. Every day he talked about the fresh air and the night sky, about how clear "It Used to Be." He told us how safe "It Used to Be," how no one bothered to lock their doors at night. And on and on.

One day, I'd had just about enough. "Why'd you leave, then?" I asked him.

He let out a deep breath and looked kind of sad. "I thought the city was where I wanted to be. I couldn't wait to get as far away as possible from the country." He kind of laughed. "Now I would love to go back."

This type of talk always made me a bit nervous.

"But you can't, right?" I asked.

Dad pulled himself out of his dream state. "Can't what, Laney?"

"Go back."

"No," he said. "I guess there's no turning back the clock."

Mom would always be listening to Dad's stories with rapture written all over her face. Probably because she grew up in New York City and barely ever saw any green grass while she was a kid. And of course Angela, the perfect one, was always getting into the stories too, sighing and acting all dreamy right along with Mom and Dad.

At exactly six o'clock I took off down the stairs and plunked myself down at the dining room table.

"What's the news?" I asked as I picked up a napkin—a cloth one, no less—and reached for a bowl of some kind of potatoes.

Mom was the one to say it. "We're moving to a ranch."

I had to concentrate with all my strength to keep from dropping that potato dish. "Moving?" I barely eked out the word.

"Oh, honey, we're so excited," Mom said. "Your father has just bought us a new home in Colorado, a little ranch where we can live and work. It's going to be wonderful!"

I set down the dish and tried to find what was left of my voice. "Colorado?" I managed to say. "Why would we ever want to leave Tampa Bay?"

For years, my dad's company had moved us all over the state of Florida. And I was supposed to be happy each time I had to start over in a new city, in a new school, with new friends. But finally the company had stopped transferring him, and I thought we had found a real home at last.

Dad was grinning almost out to his ears. "I'll show you," he said. Then he pulled out a magazine clipping from his shirt pocket and handed it to me.

I found myself staring at the weirdest-looking

animal I'd ever seen. It looked kind of like a sheep, but not really. It had a longer neck and skinnier legs. It also resembled a camel, only smaller and shaggier.

"It's an alpaca," Dad said.

Mom beamed as she fidgeted in her seat. "We're going to raise alpacas."

"We're going to raise *what*?" I screeched. "We can barely keep track of Claws!"

Claws, our only pet, was a tomcat named for the way he liked to sharpen his claws on Mom's furniture. Often he disappeared for days at a time, and we didn't know where he was or when he would return. Once, when we went to the local shelter to look for him, the people there gave us a pamphlet on "Responsible Pet Ownership." How embarrassing.

"It's going to be different out there, Laney," Dad said. "I can get out of sales and never take a business trip again. And your mom can be home every day when you and Angela get out of school."

I turned to my mom. "But I thought you liked to work."

"After fifteen years, I'm ready for a change." She leaned forward. "Listen, Laney, we're moving to Colorado, one of the most beautiful states in the country. There'll be open spaces where you can run and explore forever. You're going to love it."

The roof of my mouth turned sticky. I said to Dad,

"But we've never even seen one of these animals."

"That's true," Dad said. "But I've been doing research on the Internet and talking to people about this for a long time. Look, I also have a book." He turned around in his seat and grabbed a paperback off the counter. "These are wonderful animals. Easy to raise and keep, gentle on the land, and they produce excellent wool. It's the favorite of hand spinners and weavers."

"Very much in demand," Mom piped in, her eyes twinkling. "And they bond easily with humans. They can be almost like pets once they get to know you."

"They're from South America originally, but they're bred in the United States," Dad said. "We're getting ours from a breeder in Utah."

I crossed my arms over my chest. I couldn't believe it. I had no idea the incredible "It Used to Be" stories would ever lead to something this bizarre. I had always thought parents weren't supposed to do crazy things. I thought that territory was reserved for kids.

"We want to give you and Angela a better quality of life—the kind of childhood I had, before it's too late," Dad said, loosening his tie. Mom's pot roast was so tough he had to cut it into baby-sized pieces just to get it down his throat. He gulped hard. "We're leaving the fast lane. We're going to simplify."

Mom said, "We'll all work together, make a living the old-fashioned way."

"And exactly how will we make a living on an alpaca ranch?" I demanded.

Dad grinned. "We're going to shear and sell the wool. We'll also breed the alpacas and sell the *crias,* the offspring."

Angela, who had remained silent up to this point, was calmly cutting her meat into perfect little pieces. "Someday I may get my own horse."

Just as I had suspected. "You knew about this already, didn't you?"

A look that said "Oops" spread over Angela's face.

"Now, honey," Mom began. "We told Angela because she's older, after all, and—well, we knew she would be excited about the idea."

I stared into the darkest parts of my mom's eyes. "Well, that's just great. Everybody knew about this except for me."

Angela looked at me as if I were a poor, injured animal. "Don't take it personally, Laney."

I wanted to throw the potato dish, whatever it was, right into my sister's face. "Well, I'm not going. The rest of you can move if you like, but you can't make me go."

"Laney, be reasonable," Dad said.

Reasonable? Why should I be? "I thought we

weren't going to move anymore."

Dad looked uncomfortable. "That's what we thought. But we never dreamed this opportunity would present itself."

"We really want this, Laney," Mom said, lowering her voice.

"Well, I don't. This may be the greatest thing for you"—I glared from Mom to Dad to Angela—"but it's the worst thing that could ever happen to me."

I shoved back my chair and ran from the table before they could say another word. I flew out the front door and headed straight for the beach.

★

I kicked off my shoes and ran across the sand to the shoreline. I dug my toes into the cool, damp sand and watched the sea foam fizzle around my feet. I stood there until the sun melted on the horizon, sinking into that faraway place where the water changed to sky. In the fading light, tiny shells glistened on the beach all around me.

I took a deep breath. Sometimes it seemed as though we had lived in every coastal town in Florida. And throughout it all, the ocean had remained the only thing I could count on. It was like an old friend, always waiting for me. I could spend hours diving into the surf and floating over the waves. I could search for shells, chase sand crabs, and draw pictures in the wet sand with my fingers.

But not anymore. My parents were moving us halfway across the country to a ranch in the middle of nowhere. To take care of some ridiculous creatures that none of us had ever even seen before.

I stuck my favorite strand of hair into my mouth and chewed on it, even though it was a habit I had often promised to break.

"Look at these long, energetic curls," Mom was always saying as she worked the comb through my hair. "Now, if we could only get rid of that one flat, wet strand." Then she would press both of her palms against my cheeks and smile into my face. "Just work on it. That's all I ask."

I had tried. But now I worked the strand between my teeth until I heard the familiar squeaking sound.

Of course *Angela* had no annoying habits. She was barely a year older than I was, but she acted like—well, like an adult. She smiled and laughed at the right moments, and everyone adored her. Even her name meant "angel."

My name didn't mean anything. *Laney.* Mom and Dad said they gave it to me because they thought it was cute, but they didn't know where it came from. Once I bought a book that supposedly contained every name on earth, and even that book didn't have *Laney* listed in it. But I did find another name in the book—the perfect name.

Merissa, meaning "of the sea."

I turned and started walking down the beach, saying *Merissa* to myself. I loved the way it sounded on my lips. *Merissa.* It even sounded like the sea, like waves hissing on hot sand. If there was anything fair about this world, I would have been given that name.

As I walked on, I reached down every so often and dipped my fingers in the foam at the water's edge. This was the only place I wanted to be. The only place I could rely on. Here, the water held me up and the waves always washed me in. The shore made a straight line, one direction and back again. I could be as scattered as the shells and never get lost.

I thought about Angela, who was good at everything—school, sports, music, art. She even did some part-time modeling for department store ads. I, on the other hand, didn't really know what I was good at yet. But that didn't bother me at the beach.

I loved the sea. They couldn't make me leave it.

But when school ended for summer vacation, that's exactly what they did.

[2]

staring
into nowhere

After four days on the road, I was so tired of being in the car that I didn't care where we were. I sat slumped over in the backseat, glaring out the window. An endless prairie stretched before me, land as flat and ordinary as a department store parking lot.

This was the ugliest place I had ever seen, the part of Colorado that I didn't even know existed. I had always thought of the state as a land of mountains. But no. My parents had moved us to the eastern part of the state, the plains. Nothing but sagebrush and rocky soil and cow patties everywhere.

Dad turned the car onto a dirt driveway. "We're here," he announced.

I looked up.

"Our new home," Mom exclaimed.

New home? This house looked ancient. It was nothing but a single-story building made out of cracked, weathered brown wood, with a concrete porch. The house stood out from the flat plain like a giant cardboard box that had accidentally fallen out of an airplane. Behind it stood an old barn and some other weather-beaten outbuildings. This so-called ranch, surrounded by the same barren, featureless land we had driven over for miles, looked as lost and alone as I felt.

The moving van pulled up behind us and came to a stop as we piled out of the car.

Inside the house, things were even worse. Fraying carpet covered the floor, carpet so thin and old that I could feel the concrete underneath my feet when I took my shoes off. Scratched wood paneling hung on the walls, and a crack split the bathroom mirror straight down the center. When I glanced at myself, I found a tall gash dividing my face.

As I wandered around, looking into the rooms, I remembered our house back in Florida and all those windows facing the ocean. I remembered how they pulled in the Florida sunlight and held it there.

In our "new" house, rubber-backed drapes hung over small windows, making every room dark. Dead fly husks and stiff moth wings had collected in every corner. Even the insects didn't want to live here.

"I know we'll need to work hard to make this a better place," Mom spoke up from behind me, "but we can redecorate. Here we'll have time to complete projects together, as a family."

I turned around and squinted at her. "Why did Dad buy this place?"

"Laney," she began, "we've put our money into the land, not the house. This is valuable property, perfect pastureland for the alpacas."

The alpacas again.

"Let's choose your bedrooms," she said to Angela and me. But Angela had already picked hers and was directing the movers to it.

I didn't care. All the rooms were the same to me anyway. Horrible, dark holes in a stupid little house.

While the movers brought in boxes and furniture, Dad rounded us up. "Let's go outside, and I'll show you the rest of the place," he said.

Mom and Angela began to follow him out the back door, but I held my ground.

"Come on, Laney," Mom said. "We want to look at it all together."

But I just said, "No way."

Instead, I went to my room and stared out the window into nowhere.

Open spaces. Yeah, barbed wire fences and patchy fields and artificially green soybean farms. Every so often, a tumbleweed rolling across the road. This wasn't the grand scenery I was told I could expect of Colorado. This land was about as exciting as a blank sheet of paper. It wasn't magical or special. It offered no surprises, no seabirds suddenly floating overhead or new shells washing up on the shore.

I couldn't look anymore. I turned away and stared at the boxes the movers had stacked along the walls of my room. Everything I loved was packed away— my books and photo albums, my favorite basketball, my snorkeling mask, all my CDs. And my seashells.

I remembered having to pack them all away. I remembered the day the moving van had arrived and how I still couldn't believe what was happening. That morning, just before we left, I had run one last time to the ocean. The surface of the water was quiet and glassy, like a mirror, reflecting the gray clouds above. Almost no waves at all. I remembered how the water gently lapped onto the sand. It had sounded almost sad, as if it were softly saying good-bye.

Dad appeared in my doorway. "Time to get to work."

"What?" I nearly shouted. "We just got here."

"Yes, but we've still got some good daylight hours left. Our supplies have already been delivered, and we've got to get started on the fence." He was serious. "Only a week before the alpacas arrive."

I groaned.

"Come on. I need your help."

I opened my mouth to launch a protest, but he had vanished before I could form the words.

When I got outside, Dad tossed me a pair of work gloves. They landed in the crook of my arm. Then he gestured around the stretch of land that separated the house from the barn. "We need to secure this whole area before the alpacas arrive."

I didn't even look up. I was too busy staring at the heavy canvas gloves. They looked like the ones the dockyard workers wore—rough and ugly.

Finally I lifted my eyes and took my first good look at our land. Our so-called valuable property was mostly flat, matted grass. Only an occasional stunted tree stood out anywhere. Behind the house stood a big gray barn and beyond that, some old sheds that looked as if they were rotting on the spot.

"We're placing these posts"—Dad pointed to a pile of long wooden poles on the ground—"and attaching wire fencing."

Great.

Dad cleared his throat. "First we have to sink the posts, about six feet apart. I've already marked the spots. Angela will show you how it works."

I pursed my lips together and stuffed my hands into the gloves. I gave Angela the sickest smile I could muster while I took my directions.

"That's a posthole digger," Angela said, pointing to some contraption leaning against the side of the house. "Dad uses that to cut a hole in the ground for each post. Then we need to carry over the post, set it in the hole, and put some dirt and rocks around the base to stabilize it." Smiling, she offered me a shovel. "It's really kind of fun. And a good workout, too!"

What did I care about a good workout? I grabbed the shovel from Angela and walked over to Mom, who stood holding a post in place. A few minutes later, Dad yelled that he was ready for another post to be brought over.

I marched over to the pile of posts and tried to lift one. It hardly budged. "I can't do this," I said.

Dad looked up. "Try rolling it on the ground, or work together with Angela."

"But the posts are heavy."

"I know, Laney. It's hard work, but you can do it."

I put a hand on my hip. "This is going to take hours."

He stopped. "Yes, it may take days." Dad adjusted the sunglasses on his nose. "I'll come over there and help if necessary. But I've got enough to do myself." He turned back to his work and jammed the posthole digger into the ground with a loud whack. "We all have to pitch in. The alpacas will be arriving soon, and we have to be ready."

I spun around and crouched down close to the ground. I pulled a post out of the pile and then started rolling it over to Dad. At the hole, I wrapped my arms around the post and lifted it, using my legs to straighten myself up.

"This is disgusting," I muttered, but I kept going until the sweat from my forehead started dripping into my eyes. It burned. I pulled off a glove and rubbed one eye. *Salty,* I thought. My sweat was salty like seawater.

I ended up moving and setting at least ten of those posts, all on my own. Then I had to help string the fencing. We had to follow this exact procedure dictated by Dad: First we rolled out the wire fencing and lined it up along the posts already in the ground. Then we nailed the fencing to the posts.

We had almost finished attaching the first roll of fencing to the posts when something stabbed me in the center of my right palm.

"OW!" I yelled. I fell back onto the ground, feet spread out before me, clutching my hand.

"What is it?" Mom cried as she rushed over to me.

"Something stuck me." It was one of the wires sticking out at the end of the roll of fencing. That wire was as sharp as an ice pick, sharp enough to go right through my glove.

"Here, let me see." Mom grabbed my hand and pried it away from my chest.

I let her pull off the glove. In the center of my palm, we found a puncture wound and a little pool of blood. I lifted my hand up so everyone could get a better look. A little river of blood ran down my hand and started to drip down my wrist and onto my arm. It was a nice effect.

"Better go get the first aid kit," Dad said from over Mom's shoulder.

Mom cleaned and bandaged my wound, and then we all went back to work. But even Angela seemed hesitant after that. She wore two pairs of gloves from then on.

"Maybe I should handle the wiring from now on," Dad concluded.

I was given Mom's job of holding the posts in place. But Mom moved the posts even slower than I had. After hours of work, we had completed only one small section of fence, not even a complete side. We kept working until the sun set down on the horizon and a chill began to creep into the air.

Finally Dad said we could stop. We dragged ourselves inside. Mom started unloading pots and pans and dishes and setting up the kitchen. Dad and

Angela began unpacking their boxes and filling their closets and dressers.

But not me. I looked around my room and stared at the things the movers had brought in. My empty desk and dresser and my bare bed. I kicked aside the suitcases and duffel bags strewn on the floor and made myself a path through the room. I touched my fingertips to the boxes, strapped tightly with packing tape, stacked along the walls. I found the box that held my sleeping bag and a pillow. I opened it up and coughed. The dust had even made its way into my boxes.

I pulled the sleeping bag and pillow out of the box, shook them out, and tossed them onto my bed. Then I stared at all the rest of my boxes.

Crossing my arms and tapping my right foot, I came to a decision. I would not unpack. I could live out of my boxes. In fact, this room suited me fine just the way it was. It looked as unsettled as I felt.

And why bother unpacking, anyway? My parents were city people. Dad had a little bit of country in him from childhood, but only enough to make him a dreamer, not smart. He and Mom weren't going to cut it out here in the outback.

I looked down at the bandage wrapped around my right hand, and I smiled. My parents couldn't even take care of their own kids out here, much less a herd of alpacas.

I could wait it out. I could wait until my parents decided to abandon this insane plan and move back to Florida. In no time at all, we'd be back near the ocean, back in Tampa Bay, where we belonged.

[3]

the
color of dirt

Boredom. Monotony like I had never imagined before. Three days after our arrival and we hadn't even received a phone call or seen anything except cattle trucks droning down the road. And every day my dad made us go outside and work on the fence.

"It has to be secure or else the alpacas will be easy prey for the packs of coyotes that roam around here," he explained.

Eventually we worked out a system. We could sink a twenty-four-foot row of fence posts and string them with wire in about an hour. But we still had a long way to go. Even after three days of work, we had finished fencing in only two sides of the pasture.

"We need to work faster," Dad said.

"Are you kidding?" I asked him.

By now, our hands were blistered from handling tools that none of us had ever used before. My mom was sunburned everywhere, even on the top of her head where she parted her hair. Angela had brushed up against a rough spot on one of the fence posts and had gotten a huge splinter in her arm, and Dad had stabbed himself with wire, just as I had, twice.

"No, I'm not kidding," he said. "Only four more days until the alpacas arrive."

I took a deep breath and gazed around me. How much more sweat did I still have to drop on this ugly slab of land? Everything around me was lifeless and the color of dirt. Even the few plants that were growing weren't really green. They were more of a dull gray. And I could see no water. Anywhere.

Out of the corner of my eye, I saw the cat chasing a tumbleweed. Claws pounced on the rolling ball of thorns and immediately cried out. He sprang back to the ground, his ears flattened, trying to figure out what went wrong.

Poor Claws. He was as lost out here as we were.

There wasn't even anywhere to go in this part of Colorado. The nearest town, Hatcher, was twenty-five miles away, and all it had was a general store, a gas station, a pizza place, a post office, and a few other buildings. It wasn't even big enough to need a traffic light. Out in different directions were some other tiny towns, but we had to take the interstate all the way to Carsonville, sixty miles away, to find actual stores and fast-food places. And even that town wasn't big enough to have tennis courts, or shopping malls, or even movie theaters.

And, of course, there was nothing at all like the ocean. No waves for riding, no beach for shell searching, no sand to run through my fingers.

I stood there watching Claws until the hum of an engine broke the silence. Out on the gravel county road that passed in front of our house, a dirt-crusted pickup truck rumbled along, kicking up a cloud of gray dust behind its wheels. I dropped the post I had been lifting and stretched out my neck to get a better look. Maybe there would actually be something interesting to see this time.

But no, it was just another rancher or farmhand passing by. Some guy wearing a sweaty cowboy hat and resting a brown elbow on the open window of his truck. As quickly as he had appeared, he was gone again, vanishing into a dusty fog.

It took twenty-two minutes for the dust to completely settle back down onto the road again. I know. I timed it.

On our fourth day in nowhere, a pickup truck pulled into our driveway. A man wearing a straw hat and dusty jeans slid out of the driver's seat and came walking over to Dad and Angela.

Dad and the man shook hands. From where I was standing, I could hear the man say something about having a cattle ranch a few miles up the road and wanting to meet his new neighbors.

How nice.

Then I noticed that someone else was with him, someone who was slinking out of the truck and heading my way. As the person approached, I could see a boy's face shaded by a cowboy hat. Great. Now I was going to have to make conversation with a real country kid, someone who looked about as weird to me as I must have looked to him.

"Do you need help?" he asked.

I went back to work. "No. Actually, I think I'm doing just fine. Thanks anyway." I started lifting up the fence post I was holding.

I could hear him breathing and for some reason, the sound annoyed me.

He said, "That post is heavy. Here, let me help."

Dad was glancing over at me, so I decided I'd better be friendly. I shrugged. "OK."

After we lifted the post into the hole and propped it up, he turned and stuck out his hand. "I'm Tim," he said. He wanted to shake hands? How countrified could you get?

"I'm Laney." I touched his hand without bothering to take off my gloves.

Tim smiled, his mouth stretching into a goofy grin. "My dad and I heard you people came here from Florida to raise alpacas."

You people? I peeled off the gloves and folded them together. "Well, yes. But it wasn't my idea."

He smiled. "Pretty weird, huh?"

I grimaced. "Like I said, it's not my idea." The nerve of him. It was OK for me to call what we were doing weird, but I didn't need to hear it from someone else.

"We've never seen one of those animals around here before."

I smirked. "That makes all of us."

His face fell. "You're kidding! You mean *you've* never seen them before? Any of you?"

I looked him squarely in the eyes, giving him his answer.

He smiled again. "That's amazing. I, I mean, we thought you guys had worked with alpacas someplace else or something."

"No." I shifted my weight to the other foot.

He kept staring at me. "Have you arranged for some people, maybe experts, to help you?"

I could feel fumes rising behind my eyeballs. If he said one more word, my brain would explode.

He kept on. "I mean, you know, it's going to be hard if you're not familiar with the animals."

Who did this guy think he was? Did he and his dad come over here just to laugh at my family? I had to shut him up. I summoned up my best country twang. "Reckon so."

Tim stared silently for what seemed like forever. Then he said, "Sorry."

I looked at the pasture. I looked for my dad, then I looked at my feet. I fixed my eyes on the dirt-caked tops of my new cross-trainers and studied the deep scrapes dug into the leather.

Tim must have been following my eyes. "You're going to need some cowboy boots out here."

I met his stare. "Cowboy boots? I don't think so."

He cocked his head to one side. "You don't want to be here, do you?"

"No," I said. "And I'm not going to be here for long, either."

Angela pulled herself away from Tim's father and came strolling toward us. She immediately took Tim under her wing, offering to show him around the place. Fine with me. She was welcome to him. He seemed as dull as the dirt around me anyway. I turned away without saying good-bye, but I doubted if either of them noticed.

I slipped around to the other side of the house, away from them all. I couldn't stand to watch Angela casting her spell on new people. And in the end, they would probably still think we were nothing but a bunch of stupid city folks.

I could just hear it. Those idiots from Florida out here to raise animals they knew nothing about. How could I ever show my face anywhere in this county?

I would have given anything to be back in Florida at that moment. To go to the ocean and feel the salt water on my skin and stand in my favorite spot until my toes sank into the sand. If only I could hear and smell the water, chase a wave, dig inside a dune.

I noticed a ladder propped up against the house. I paused for a second. Then I climbed up. I carefully crawled over the weather-beaten shingles and perched myself in the middle of the roof. I looked as far into the distance as possible.

I tried to remember what it had been like to climb to the highest point of a sand dune and strain my eyes to see the gulls nesting out on the narrow spits of land offshore.

But from our roof, all I could see was the enormous nothingness that surrounded me. Wherever Tim's ranch was, it was too far away to be seen from up here. The road disappeared in both directions into shimmering heat mirages. The only other things I could pick out were a field dotted with black and brown cows, a stack of hay, and some strange rock formations off to the east.

I frowned. Those rocks. I had noticed them on our first day here, and now I spotted something else. Was that a windmill among them? I stood up and edged along the roof until I could get a better view. Then I spied something even more interesting nestled in the rocks. It was a small turquoise trailer.

★

"I thought we didn't have any close neighbors," I said that night at dinner.

Mom and Dad glanced at each other with confused looks. "Well, none to speak of," Dad said. "What do you mean, Laney? Have you seen something we don't know about?"

"A trailer, in the rocks," I said.

Recognition spread over Angela's face. "That must be the woman Tim told me about." She took a bite of the chicken stew Dad had cooked. As she chewed, disgust spread over her face, but she quickly put on a half smile and set her spoon down.

The home cooking experiment wasn't going so

well. My parents could have easily opened one of those camps where people go to lose weight. No one would eat this food. Even Angela regularly snitched chips and cookies out of the kitchen pantry just to survive.

Angela finished chewing. "A woman lives there alone. She's the county weirdo, a misfit. But she's harmless, according to Tim."

This was classic Angela. Her all-knowing air, the tone of familiarity she used when she said "Tim," as if they had been friends for years.

"Misfit?" Mom laughed. "Oh, she couldn't be that bad. If she's our neighbor, we should be friendly."

Dad looked at me. "You could go visit sometime, if you want." He gave me a little nod.

I pushed the stew around with my spoon. "No, I don't think so."

That's just what I needed—to be paired up with the county weirdo. The family misfit with the county misfit.

No way.

[4]

the
arrival

On the day the alpacas were coming, I woke up with a little jump. Then I turned over, pulled the pillow down over my head, and tried to drift back to sleep.

But a thud on the door jolted me out of it.

"Come on. Time to get ready," Mom announced.

I pressed the pillow against my ears and tried to ignore everything except my need to sleep again. But I could still hear the footsteps clumping up and down the hallway and Dad's voice outside near the barn, punching holes in the quiet morning air.

Finally I forced myself out of bed.

Mom and Dad had awakened early and dressed in jeans, denim work shirts, and leather boots, clothes they had bought at the western-wear shop in Carsonville. Dad also had on a cowboy hat that he'd started to wear outside to prevent sunburn, or so he said. But to me, he just looked like a businessman dressed up as a cowboy for Halloween.

Dad directed Angela and me to sweep out the barn. Then we had to break up large bales of fresh straw with a pitchfork and spread the straw around with a rake. Meanwhile, Mom carried in bags of grain pellets, a supplement to the alpacas' diet of grass and hay, and stacked the bags on shelves. Dad hung new plastic feed pails on hooks.

Then Dad made us follow him as he took one last circle around the pasture, checking the fence. Somehow we had managed to close off a huge area behind the house, up to and including the barn. We had hung a large metal gate on the section of the fence closest to the house, just past the end of our driveway. Beyond the pasture, we had converted one of the old outbuildings into a storage shed. The other two outbuildings were so infested with mice and close to collapsing that Dad had decided to tear them down.

Dad looked around the pasture and took a deep breath. "Guess we're ready." He pulled his hat down on his brow. "You and Angela run fresh drinking water into the trough."

After we finished the last of the preparations, I climbed up high on the pasture gate, where I had a clear view all around us. Then I waited. Angela pulled up a lawn chair on the front porch and sat down to read the latest issue of her new horse magazine. Mom stood around on one foot and then the other, while Dad stared up the road and frequently checked his watch.

The sun beat down on us. Even the wind was still, as if it were waiting for something, too.

As I stared up the road, looking for the now familiar cloud of dust that always came before any vehicle, my eyes wandered to the rocks. I wanted nothing to do with the weirdo who lived among them, but there was something interesting about the stones themselves. I was hoping to explore the formations as soon as I could.

So far, though, I hadn't had a chance. Every day Mom and Dad had found something "of dire importance" for me to do. If we weren't working on the fence, we were applying sealant to the roof of the barn. We had cleaned the cobwebs and rats' nests out of the storage shed. We had hung the metal gate that led to the pasture. And we had started tearing down the two infested outbuildings.

Then every night, after a full day's work, Dad made us listen to him as he read out loud from his alpaca book. His new purpose in life was to make us memorize every aspect of alpaca care.

I hadn't had one moment to myself.

But, at the very least, this day would be different. Finally I would see the dreaded animals that were responsible for ruining my life. As the moments crept by, I passed the time by swinging on the gate, back and forth, pushing off the ground with the tips of my toes.

At last, a king cab truck came rolling down the road with a livestock trailer hitched to the back of it. The trailer weaved slightly from side to side. When the truck pulled to a stop in our driveway, Dad walked over to greet the driver. They entered into a long discussion about how to unload the animals.

While they talked, Mom and Angela tiptoed up to the trailer. I wanted to look, too. Just one look, just a peek at the creatures who had taken me away from the ocean and changed all of our lives. That's all I wanted. I strode up to the trailer, scowling.

The smell of manure hit me. I peered between the slats of the trailer. Loud shuffling and banging sounds came from within. I saw darting black eyes and heard something like a child's cry. Slowly, I backed away.

Mom and Angela continued to peek from the other side. "They are soooo cute!" Angela squealed.

The truck driver glanced in our direction. "It's probably best if you stay away, for now." Then he hopped into his truck and began backing it up to the pasture gate. He had some trouble maneuvering around a big boulder and a couple of potholes and couldn't back all the way up to the gate. But finally, when he had gotten the trailer as close as he could, he climbed out of the truck, took a deep breath, and lowered the tailgate.

Terrified animals lurched forward and stepped on each other as they piled down the ramp of the trailer. The driver tried to push the first few alpacas through the gate and into the pasture while Dad stood by, looking as confused as the animals did.

"Oh dear," Mom said, clasping her hands together.

The first two alpacas stumbled into the pasture. But the next two alpacas halted at the end of the ramp and turned, slipping between the truck and the fence. They looked about frantically for a place to go. Mom approached one of them and said, "There, there." She tried to pet it like a dog.

The alpaca arched back and spit a wad of phlegm on Mom's new shirt. She screamed. Then the alpaca took off, heading toward the horizon.

I didn't know what to do. Mom was gagging at the sight of green mucus on her shirt, so Dad yelled at me to go after the wayward alpaca. I took off and tried to catch up with the escapee, a large pinkish-tan creature, but I couldn't get anywhere near it. I just ran along, gasping and choking on its dust.

Finally the alpaca slowed down, and I came up alongside of it. The animal stopped, stood at attention, and looked at me with one wild, suspicious eye. I was panting through my nose and mouth at the same time. Then I moved nearer, but the alpaca snorted, reared back, and lifted up its front legs.

At that instant I realized I had come too close to the beast. I prepared myself to get blasted with green phlegm. But instead, the alpaca came back down with one outstretched leg, stepping on top of my cross-trainer. "OW!" I yelled. Then, just to make sure he had gotten his point across, he stomped on my foot again.

Mom raced toward me, her face full of fear. The phlegm was running down the front of her shirt. "Are you hurt?" she cried out.

"No, I'm OK," I answered. But those toenails, or whatever was on the bottom of the alpaca's foot, sure were hard.

The animal took off again. Mom and I chased after him as he led us around in circles and occasionally tried to bolt for the hazy horizon. Finally we got behind him and yelled and drove him back to the pasture gate.

Just outside the gate, Dad and Angela were chasing down the other escapee, a big white one. Dad got the alpaca turned around toward the pasture. But he moved in too close. The alpaca bucked backward, landing a solid blow on Dad's shin. Dad stumbled forward, holding on to his leg with both hands, his face bright red and ready to burst. Mom rushed to his aid while I looked to the driver for help. *Please don't desert us,* I pleaded with my eyes. *It's obvious we don't know what we're doing.*

The driver helped Angela and me drive more of the alpacas from the livestock trailer into the pasture, keeping as much distance from them as possible. The alpacas' eyes were wild with fright, and we certainly didn't want to get kicked like Dad. He was still doubled over with pain, and Mom was checking for broken bones.

Somehow we managed to get all the remaining alpacas out of the trailer and into the pasture. But the Kicker was still on the loose. Now he decided to go for a little jog. Angela and I chased the beast until Angela doubled over with a cramp. Dad, limping on his injured leg, tried to step in for her, but he wasn't much help.

Shaking his head, the truck driver decided to put us out of our misery. He obviously couldn't wait to finish this job and leave. He flung himself in front of the Kicker and began to shoo and scare the creature until it turned and ran for its life. Hollering and waving his arms, he drove the Kicker toward the pasture until the animal bolted through the gate.

At last all the alpacas stood inside the pasture, amid choking clouds of dust and pathetic cries. The truck driver got his papers signed as quickly as possible, climbed into his truck, and disappeared down the road.

I looked at Mom, Dad, and Angela, all of whom seemed to have lost their ability to speak. Then I looked at the strange scene inside our perfectly fenced pasture. I climbed up onto the gate and studied the alpacas.

These were weird-looking animals. They were about three feet tall and had thick, shaggy coats, full bodies, and long, thin necks. Their legs were skinny, and instead of hooves, they had padded feet with two large toenails. Toenails I was already quite familiar with, thank you very much.

There were twenty alpacas in the herd. That seemed to me like a lot to start out with, especially for amateurs like us, but my father had insisted on diving right in. The animals stood huddled together in the center of the pasture, as if they wanted to be as far away from us humans as possible. Every few minutes one of the alpacas stomped its foot and glared sideways at us. Poor dumb animals. They didn't want to be here any more than I did.

They were supposed to be tame and sociable. That's what Dad's book had said. They were supposed to be halter trained and loving toward their caretakers, almost like pets. And they were only supposed to get aggressive, spitting and kicking, when treated harshly.

Ha. So much for the information in Dad's book.

As the sun spread out across the late-afternoon sky, the alpacas finally seemed to calm down. The tension slipped out of their necks, and with their fleece glowing in the light of the sunset, they looked almost peaceful.

"We'll just have to work with them, that's all," Dad said that night at dinner. "Get them to trust us." Just in from the barn, he looked horrible. His hair dripped with sweat, and dust had collected in the fine lines that spread across his forehead. He looked into his plate and took a slow bite of pizza.

Mom, back to her old ways already, had broken down and driven all the way to Hatcher for a couple of pepperoni pizzas. They were cold by the time she got home, but we were too hungry and tired to care.

"It will get better," Mom said, trying to sound cheerful. But she wouldn't look directly at Angela or me. Instead she pushed the hair off her face, picked

41

up a slice of pizza, and devoured a big piece of pepperoni hanging off the edge.

After minutes of heavy silence, Dad looked up at me. "How's your foot?"

I tried to hide my smile. "It's sore." That was the truth. The alpaca did hurt me. But I didn't mind. It was another good reason to hate the beasts. I reached down and rubbed the top of my foot. "It'll be OK."

Dad had been limping ever since he got kicked. "My leg is killing me," he said.

Mom spoke quickly. "I'm sorry you're hurt, but that's the least of our problems."

Dad dropped his napkin in his plate and sat back. "OK, go ahead and say it."

"Say what?" Mom asked, playing dumb.

"Say what's on your mind."

"I'm sure I don't know what you mean."

"Right."

They stopped. Like it suddenly dawned on them that they were fighting in front of us, something they rarely did. Mom cleared her throat and looked back at Dad. "The driver informed me that the alpacas haven't completed their immunizations."

Dad nodded. "I knew that already. The immunizations aren't due yet. We have time to do it."

I glanced at my sister. Her eyebrows flew upward. "We?" she asked. "You don't mean we have to give them shots?" Even Angela could see that we were not in any way ready to do anything like this to animals that had just nearly managed to kill us.

Mom plastered the smile back on her face. "Of course not. We'll get a veterinarian to do it."

No one responded, not even Dad. Finally he said, "I guess I'll find a vet for the alpacas, and then I'll find a doctor for me." He shoved his plate forward, stood up, and limped away from the table.

I could barely contain myself. This was great—my parents were never going to be able to handle these animals or life out here in the middle of nowhere. They couldn't control the alpacas, they couldn't cook, and the house was a mess. Dishes with petrified ketchup and drying eggs sat in the kitchen sink. Dirty footprints and clods of grass marked the floor. Dust covered everything. Somehow I didn't think this was exactly the "It Used to Be" that my dad had been hoping to re-create.

I remembered an old saying, *Look before you leap.* Too bad my parents hadn't done that. Today's events could only be called a disaster. But I couldn't have been happier. I would be back in Florida before school started.

That night, as I curled into bed, I imagined diving into the ocean and floating on my back like a seal.

[5]

into
the rocks

A few days later, Mom and Dad sat at the breakfast table poring over a shopping list.

"We're all taking a day off from work," Dad announced.

"Today we're going to the Kmart in Carsonville," Mom said.

Dad looked up at me, his eyelids drooping as I'd never seen them before. "We need a break."

Mom glanced at me. "Come with us. It'll be fun."

I gave her my best numb stare. "No thanks."

Angela perked up. "I'm going along to pick out new curtains for the living room and wallpaper for the kitchen."

Of course she was. Of course Angela would be helping my parents redecorate the house. And learning everything about the alpacas. And going along with everything my parents said and did.

I jumped up, grabbed a bottle of water from the refrigerator, and headed out the door. I didn't slow down until I reached the gravel road.

I glanced from side to side as I passed yellow grass and stiff plants that somehow grew in the dead soil along the side of the road. I crossed a dry creek bed—a *wash,* it was called. It was about fifteen feet wide and lined with pale dirt, patches of juniper, and clumps of sagebrush. The wash didn't hold a single drop of water.

When the house was far behind me, lost in the dust, I came to a narrow drive. Two stripes of dirt lined with tire tracks veered away from the road in the direction of the rock formations.

I stopped. The sun beat down on my neck, and little beads of sweat started to form on my forehead. I took a long drink of water and stared up the drive. I figured it led to the trailer where the weird lady lived, somewhere among the rocks.

These rocks looked different from the other big rocks I'd seen around here. I really wanted to get a closer look at them.

I turned and walked up the drive, stepping softly.

I knew I'd have to be quiet if I wanted to come and go without being seen.

As I drew nearer, I could see that the rocks stood in an almost perfect circle, forming a protected, private enclosure.

I walked closer. The windmill loomed overhead just beyond the rocks, its blades barely looping around in the almost still air. I paused and listened. Except for the occasional squeak of the windmill, everything was silent.

I crept up to the first huge stone. Reaching out to touch it, I let the air come slowly out of my lungs. On the surface of the stone was a warm, grainy layer of sand. It was sandstone—ancient sea sand hardened into stone. I had seen this kind of rock once when we were on vacation in Arizona.

I let my palm glide along the surface as I walked around the huge stone. I came to the place where it met a second boulder. Between the two rocks I found a narrow passageway filled with deep shadows. The air smelled rich and moist, and tiny green plants grew on the ground. There was just enough room for me to slip in between the stones. I leaned back against the cool rock. Its surface was damp and grainy, and for a second I thought I smelled the beach. I closed my eyes and let my mind wander.

I tried to picture the ocean, but instead, images

of sagebrush and dirt loomed before me. I couldn't push them away. It was as if this weird new place was starting to invade my memory banks. Could I already be forgetting my ocean?

A small noise broke the silence. My eyes popped open. It sounded like a footstep. I stood perfectly still and listened, but I heard nothing more. Keeping my back flat against the stone, I slithered further in between the rocks and stole a peek inside the circle.

An old woman with an odd gait was approaching, rocking from side to side. This woman wobbled like a see-saw. I pressed myself back into the rock and silently prayed that she wouldn't see me. But as her raspy breathing grew louder, drawing nearer, I knew I had been discovered. Slowly I pushed myself away from the rock and stepped out of the shadows.

"Who are you?" the woman blurted out as she approached me.

I tried to smile. "I live in the house down the road. I just came to see the rocks."

"Aahhh," the woman said. She stopped rocking and, with both hands, rubbed the small of her back. "I knew I didn't recognize you."

"Sorry to startle you."

"No, you didn't. It takes a sight more than that to startle me. Well, come on up." She motioned for me to follow her.

I took a step backward. "No, I … I really should get back," I stammered.

"Nonsense," she said. "The rest of your family is gone, left a few minutes ago, up the road in that nice station wagon."

That struck me. "How did you know?"

The woman smiled. I shaded my eyes and took a good look at her. She had quick, bright eyes and a round face framed with gray-brown curls that stuck out from under a tattered straw hat. She wasn't nearly as old as I had first thought.

She said, "Well, there aren't too many folks out here, in case you didn't notice. In these parts, we keep an eye on each other."

I forced a smile back onto my face and bit my lip. She seemed nice enough, but I really didn't feel like making conversation with this woman. As I stood there trying to come up with an excuse to leave, she spoke again.

"We haven't been properly introduced," she said, reaching out her hand.

That handshaking thing again.

"I'm M.J. My real name is Marjorie Jane, but it never seemed to fit me, so I shortened it to M.J. years ago." Creases formed around the outside corners of her eyes, and her teeth gleamed in the sunshine. "Most people call me the Birdhouse Lady."

I let my shoulders fall, doomed. I would have to stay for at least a brief conversation or be considered unbelievably rude.

"I'm Laney," I said, taking M.J.'s hand.

"You can call me M.J. or the Birdhouse Lady. Doesn't matter much to me either way." She squeezed my hand for a few seconds. Then she smiled again. "I'm surely pleased to meet you, Laney. Come on, I'll show you around." Slowly, she started rocking up toward the trailer.

I had no choice but to follow.

"Now, what's this?" the woman murmured, gesturing to my water bottle. "Some of that designer water?"

I held it up. "I guess."

"Mm-hmm. Very popular these days," she said between steps. "Never touch the stuff myself."

"Why not?"

"Well, why should I?" Another step. "I get all the water I need." She nodded in the direction of the windmill.

As we walked, I took in everything around me. A different world—a cluttered, busy, green world—lay inside the circle of rocks. Flowering geraniums grew in rusted iron pots. Honeysuckle vines twisted around the bases of fruit trees, blooming lilac bushes and brown-faced sunflowers grew in flower beds, and beyond the windmill, I could see a vegetable garden staked out in rows.

And that trailer. It was turquoise, just as I had noticed from our roof, but it was older than I had imagined, bullet-shaped and teetering high off the ground on concrete blocks. Wooden steps led up to a small platform and a door. Beside the trailer sat a faded blue pickup truck with a gray tailgate. The driver's-side door was painted white.

My eyes traveled back to the windmill. "You really get your water from the windmill?"

"Actually, from a well," M.J. replied. "But the windmill does the pumping."

"Oh," I said.

M.J. nodded toward my water bottle again. "That's recyclable, you know."

"Yeah, I know." I immediately felt heat collecting under my skin. I didn't have a clue what to say, and what was I doing here, anyway?

As we walked on, M.J.'s chest heaved up and down with each step. We moved past an oddball assortment of sheds, a rusted washing machine, and an old watering trough filled with tomato plants. When we reached the trailer steps, M.J. rested, took a deep breath, and smiled as about twenty cats emerged from underneath the trailer. The cats cried and stretched and made circles around us. About ten of them followed as M.J. slowly led me up the steps and through the door.

Inside, the trailer was so small that two people couldn't pass each other without colliding. Stuffed with sagging furniture and stacks of old books and magazines, it looked and smelled as if it hadn't tasted fresh air for years. An oil lamp and a stack of dirty dishes sat on a chipped Formica table, and crusty cat food bowls were scattered around the floor.

Now seemed like as good a time as any to try to make my getaway. But I found I no longer had the urge. I stepped around the cat food bowls and sat down at the table across from M.J., the Birdhouse Lady, or whoever she was.

M.J. took off her hat. "So you're my new neighbor." She cocked her head to one side and stared at me with bright blue eyes that seemed to look right into the very center of me.

I began crossing the tips of my shoes over and over each other. "My parents gave up their city jobs in Florida and came out here to raise alpacas."

"W-e-l-l-l," M.J. said, drawing that short word out to at least three syllables. "Good for them." She stared directly into my pupils now. "Good for them," she said again, softer this time.

"They like it, and so does my older sister, Angela. Of course, she likes *everything*." I rolled my eyeballs.

M.J. raised her right brow at me.

"But I hate it here," I continued.

A black thing pounced on the table. The sudden movement made me jump into the air like a flying fish. But it was only one of the cats, a big black tom. He arched his back and butted his face against M.J.'s shoulder, purring so loudly he sounded like one of those riding lawn mowers on the golf courses back in Florida.

M.J. scratched under the cat's chin. "Oh, what a big baby. Mama's baby," she cooed, slowly stroking his spine. She looked back up at me. "You hate it here, you say?"

I nodded. I found my favorite strand of hair and stuck it into my mouth.

M.J. studied me. "But you like my rocks?" she asked with a smile.

I let myself relax a little and sat back in the chair. "It's because they're made of sand. They remind me of where I used to live—the beach."

"You don't say." M.J. raised her eyebrow again. "You know, this whole part of the country was once covered by a shallow sea."

I shrugged. What did it matter? I didn't care what this place looked like a million years ago. I cared about what it looked like now, and that was ugly.

"Oh yes," M.J. replied. "You can even find fossils

of ancient clams, but only if you know where to look." She pushed the cat to one side. "I'll take you there sometime, if you wish."

I blinked hard, suddenly shy again. At that moment, a yellow cat sprang up onto the table. Then more came, arching and purring, each vying for attention. It was impossible to ignore the furry animals. I started cooing and scratching them right along with M.J. Two more pounced on the table, and M.J. laughed out loud, a cackle that reminded me of a seabird.

Later we went back outside so she could show me her garden. We inspected rows of herbs, bean vines, and vegetables. We visited her scarecrow, which was made entirely of trash. A plastic milk bottle stuck on top of an old broom handle served as the head and body. His legs and arms were made of empty aluminum cans strung together. They swayed whenever a breeze made its way into the circle of rocks, making him look as if he were moon-walking.

I suddenly remembered to ask, "Why does everyone call you the Birdhouse Lady?"

M.J. chuckled. She rocked over to check her tomato plants. "Because I make birdhouses. Sometimes I need a little money." M.J. leaned over and pushed down on the sticks that held the plants upright. "Can't quite grow everything I need here, so

I build birdhouses and sell them. I do a pretty good business, especially at the county fair." She smiled and let out a deep breath. "And besides, I love to make them."

I tried to imagine what kind of birdhouses M.J. made. They would have to be different, not anything like the ones in stores. "May I see one?"

M.J. headed toward the bean vines. "You could if I had any. I'm clean out right now." She stopped, turned, and looked at me. "I noticed you're tearing down two of those old sheds on your property. Any plans for the old wood?"

I shook my head. Dad had left the wood piled up in two stacks. "I think my dad was planning to burn it whenever he got the chance."

"Oh no," she said. "Don't do that. That's like chopping down a tree for no reason. I'll take any old wood, anytime." She wiped her hands on her skirt. "I'll come pick it up next chance I get."

M.J. worked her way through the garden, checking plants and pulling up weeds. I found myself wanting to ask questions. How could M.J. support herself making birdhouses? How could she survive out here all alone? She had nothing nice, nothing that wasn't old or recycled at least once. She didn't even use running water or electricity.

"Oil lamps work fine for lighting," she explained

later when I asked her how she managed. "I have the woodstove for heat. And I'm not alone. Look at all this company I have." She gestured to all the cats lazing in the sunshine. "Besides, if you're lonely when you're alone, then you're in bad company—a French philosopher once said that."

When M.J. milked the cow, an old swaybacked creature named Chamomile, I stood by and watched as the big tin bucket slowly filled up with fresh milk. Then we stepped down into the cool darkness of the ice cellar, where M.J. stored her food. Huge cubes of ice made the place feel like the frozen food aisle at the grocery store. Along the walls, racks held tubs of homemade butter and fresh eggs.

"My food is better than any of that stuff in those fancy markets. Haven't been in one for years," M.J. said to me.

When we explored the henhouse, the chickens squawked their disapproval. A fat white hen flew up and nearly landed on my head. I had to duck quickly and dart sideways to get out of its way.

M.J. cackled again. "A girl like you has a lot to get used to out here. Maybe I can help." She looked up at me with sparkling eyes. "Come visit me and my rocks anytime."

Suddenly M.J. grabbed her right side. A pained expression drained her face.

I opened my mouth, but before I could speak, M.J. breathed out and said, "Scoliosis."

I nodded even though I didn't have a clue what scoliosis was.

"Curvature of the spine. Had it since birth. Only bothers me every so often."

I nodded again as I realized that this condition must explain her strange rocking gait and her difficulty breathing. She had looked uncomfortable the whole time I had been with her. Yet she had never complained.

At sunset, I finally left the circle of rocks. As I walked away from the trailer, M.J. stood on the wooden platform outside her door, waving me off. "When the electricity gets blown out this winter, you can come over here and get warm by the woodstove," she called.

"OK," I shouted over my shoulder. "As long as I don't have to bring my sister!"

M.J. laughed and waved furiously at me. I turned back once more to look at her standing there alone.

At that moment, alone sounded great. Maybe someday I could live by myself in a trailer on the beach, tucked away in a hidden cove, with no one but the seagulls and the sand crabs for company. I'd live as M.J. did, perfectly happy to be by myself.

But as I walked on, the strange sounds and scents

of the prairie coming alive in the night air brought me back to where I was. They made me even more homesick for the heavy wet air of the ocean, the salty smells, and the sea breezes.

I took the rest of the walk back home one slow step at a time. As the lights of the house drew nearer, I had to force myself to keep going. Climbing the steps to the front porch, my shoes felt so heavy I'd swear their soles were made of cement.

[6]

frozen in headlights

I thought my chores would get easier once the fence was done and the alpacas arrived. But no. They became even worse. Every day my parents forced me into hours of manual labor.

Mom banged on my bedroom door early each morning before the sun was even all the way up. I rolled out of bed and staggered to the shower. Then I dressed for a day in the hot sun and went outside to tackle my chores.

First, Angela and I had to feed and water the alpacas. Using a wide stick, I would skim off all the dead gnats and moths that floated on the surface of the alpacas' water trough. Every few minutes, I'd have to stop and bat away the flies that swarmed around my head. They seemed to just love my long curls. Lucky me. Then we would bring the hose around and refill the trough with fresh water.

After that, we had to dump all the old feed out of the feeding trough. We'd fill a pail with fresh, new, pasty-colored pebbles, lug it over, and pour it into the trough, turning our faces so we wouldn't inhale a lungful of dust. We did this over and over again until the trough was filled to the correct level according to Dad. And to make matters worse, it was all a waste of time anyway. The alpacas rarely ate any of the pellets or hay we put out for them. Dad insisted we keep trying to feed them new things. But they seemed to prefer grazing on the natural vegetation, or maybe they just didn't want to eat anything that had been touched by human hands.

We still couldn't get within ten feet of the alpacas. Every morning, as soon as Angela and I slipped through the gate to water and feed them, the entire herd would move to the farthest corner of the pasture. In the evenings, when the animals seemed their calmest, Dad would come out with a halter and try to strap it onto one of them, always unsuccessfully.

One night Dad got within a few feet of a big brown female that Angela called Chocolate. But all of a sudden Chocolate scuttled away and looked back at Dad as if she wanted to spit at him. After that she wouldn't let him get close to her again.

I sometimes worried that M.J. would drop by for a visit and witness one of these scenes. I was sure I would die of embarrassment if she did. I couldn't take another humiliating experience like the one with the alpaca truck driver. Or the one with Tim and his father. I didn't want anyone else to see that my parents' precious alpacas couldn't even stand the sight of us.

Since there was nothing we could do with the animals, Dad found all kinds of other projects for us to do. We painted the barn red and finished tearing down the two infested outbuildings, all the way to the ground. We wallpapered the kitchen and bathroom. Every night, when I stretched out in my bed, my back ached. And even though I had worn gloves constantly, the blisters on my hands had turned into hard calluses.

One day, while I was filling the trough with food pellets that probably wouldn't get eaten, I glanced over at the alpacas. They were looking at me sideways, suspiciously, like they always did. All except for one, a female with a pinkish-tan coat that Dad called fawn-colored. This alpaca was staring at me dead on, as if she was trying to tell me something.

I put my hand on one hip and regarded her for a

moment. The angle, the way she was standing, made me notice something. From this viewpoint I could see her sides bulging out. She was downright fat. Either fat or something else. Maybe pregnant.

As soon as Dad came over from the barn, I pointed it out to him. "Don't you think she looks bigger than the others?" I asked him.

Dad took off his cowboy hat and wiped his brow with the back of one hand. Putting the hat back on, he squinted at the alpaca.

"She *is* bigger. I don't think I would have noticed, the way they huddle up against each other all the time." He turned to me. "She might be pregnant. Good thing you saw it, Laney."

I felt my heart begin to speed up. Just what we needed. A pregnant alpaca meant another hateful animal to take care of soon. I swung the empty feed pail up on my arm and walked away.

After I finished mucking out the barn and spreading fresh straw, I decided to walk down to M.J.'s place. I wanted to tell her that Dad had agreed to give her the wood from the two old sheds and that he'd drive it over to her as soon as he could. And besides, visiting M.J. would at least give me something to do. Anything was better than hanging out at our place looking at nothing.

On the road, the stillness was so thick that it felt

heavy against my skin. I stopped and shielded my eyes from the sun, looking out to the eastern horizon. Then I turned and looked in the other direction.

Vastness. Unbroken, open vastness. No buildings or people, no cars to dodge, nothing. And silence. Only the sounds of insects and the wind. In this quietness, it was impossible not to think, not to let your mind wander.

Was being in the middle of this big open prairie like being a castaway in the middle of the ocean? I started thinking about Florida. I wondered what the water looked like today. Foamy and green, or calm and blue? I wondered what new shells had washed up on the shore. I wondered if I'd ever see the ocean again.

My eyes landed on something up ahead, jarring me back to reality. Something big and brown lay along the side of the road. I stopped for a minute, straining to see. It looked like a dead animal.

Closing in, I recognized a deer. Not the white-tailed kind, but the other kind—large, with big ears and bulky bodies. Mule deer, that was the name. A smell similar to rotting fish hung in the air.

The deer had probably been dead for some time. Tiny gnats and flies buzzed and landed, flew away and then returned, feeding on the carcass. I moved around to the head of the deer and stared at the face. The mouth gaped open, revealing a dry, pink tongue. The eyes bulged out, wide with fright.

Obviously a car or truck had hit this animal. I fought off a wave of nausea as I studied those pathetic, blank eyes staring in terror at nothing. I blinked back tears. Even though I was repulsed by it, I stayed and looked at that deer for a long time.

When I couldn't look any longer, I stepped past the carcass and slowly walked away.

★

"There's a dead deer on the road," I told M.J.

"That so?" she said as she settled into the dinette. "Happens all the time around here, I'm afraid."

"Really? Well, whatever killed that animal must have been going pretty fast. The deer looked like it never even knew what hit it."

"Actually, it probably did," replied M.J. "That's the worst part. A deer freezes in a car's headlights. Poor thing's so stunned by the light that it can't even move out of the way."

"But that's horrible!"

"Yes, it is," M.J. said, shaking her head. "Sad. They used to run freely over open territory. But now they must cross roads and highways, and it isn't safe for them anymore."

A sudden anger coursed through my veins. I

couldn't help thinking about my parents, who chose to care for animals who weren't even native to this continent when other animals were dying right outside their doorway. Not animals brought here and set to pasture. Animals that *belonged* here.

And what a terrible way to die. Waiting, frozen on the road, for some car or truck to mow you down. That was even worse than a blind curve. These deer could actually see the danger coming.

"Well, not much use dwelling on it, I suppose," M.J. said. "Funny, you showing up like this. I was just on my way to your place."

"Oh, no." I sat up straight. "You don't have to come over. My dad says he'll bring the wood to you as soon as he gets a chance."

M.J. waved off the idea. "That's nice of him, but I had my mind all set to haul wood today." She cleared the dishes from the table. "I'll just drop on by and pick it up. It'll give me a chance to see those alpacas of yours, anyway."

"No!" I said a bit too forcefully as the image of Dad chasing Chocolate around with the halter came back to me. "Dad wants to wash the wood down and let it dry out first. He'll bring it himself. Really."

"Sure enough?" M.J. rubbed her chin. "Well, OK, then. But I'm eager to get started on those birdhouses. Guess I'll have to go out hunting."

"For what?"

"More wood. People from all over this county save their wood for me to make my birdhouses. They leave word at the nearest general store when they have some." M.J. looked up at me. "You can come with me, if you like."

Out in the truck, it took ten minutes for M.J.'s engine to turn over. "Only take her out once or twice a month, so she's a little stubborn," M.J. said with a wink.

Finally we took off, bouncing up and down on the rutted road. The truck had something I had never seen before—a three-speed manual transmission on the steering column.

"Don't think they make them like this anymore," M.J. said as she thrust the stick up and down.

After about thirty minutes of driving, M.J. finally rolled the truck to a stop in the center of a one-street, two-tree town, one I hadn't been in before. It was almost identical to Hatcher, except that there was a bank and a boarded-up movie theater across from the general store.

A couple of old men sat in the shade on a park bench. Both of them waved, and the chubby one slowly chewed on something inside his cheek as M.J. and I walked by.

Inside the general store, M.J. vanished into the

back room with a man who wore a stained white apron. I waited at the counter and let the breeze from an electric fan dry my forehead. Then I glanced around.

The weirdest assortment of items filled the place. Everything from horse tack to chicken feed to Broncos T-shirts. There were pots and dishes, toys and birthday cards, costume jewelry and chocolate candy, all under one roof.

I walked down the first aisle. The old wooden-plank floor creaked with each step. Did they have anything new here? Some of this stuff looked as if it had been sitting around since World War II.

Then I spotted a display of CDs. I flew over and began flipping through the stack. But there wasn't one single singer or group that I knew. I shifted my weight and started to search through another stack.

"May I help you?" someone asked me.

I looked up at a woman with silver hair and glasses on a chain around her neck. I picked out a CD and turned it over. "Do you have anything besides country-western?"

"Oh no," the woman said. "Not anymore. We once carried a few classical CDs, but they didn't sell very well."

I tried to smile. Unbelievable. No popular groups or new music. "Thanks anyway," I said.

M.J. finally emerged from the back room, chattering and slowly making her way to the front of the store. I rushed to open the door and get us out of there as quickly as possible.

"Got some," M.J. said as she lumbered into the driver's seat. "The Grants just dismantled an old shed. Next stop: Grants' ranch."

As we drove along, we passed fields and farmhouses, rusting farm machinery and weathered wood buildings, bales of hay and red barns.

"Yes," M.J. answered herself out of the blue, "making birdhouses is fitting with my philosophy, seeing as I'm into recycling and all. Don't want to add any more trash to this beautiful world."

Within an hour, we arrived at the ranch—a huge piece of land, a sprawling house, and a collection of mismatched buildings. The Grants, people who looked completely at home in their western clothes, shook M.J.'s hand and led us to a stack of old wood. Standing over the pile, M.J. put on her glasses—two half-moons of plastic held together with an old Band-Aid.

Slowly M.J. ran her hands over the planks. "These will do just fine," she said, looking pleased. "Just fine, indeed." She handed them one by one to me. Then I carried them to the truck and stacked them in the back.

After M.J. pumped the Grants' hands over and over and said thank you in every possible way, we took off again. We puttered along, while M.J. told me funny things that had happened to her since she'd lived within those sandstone rocks. Like the time she found a rattlesnake curled up and napping in her outhouse.

"Had to prod him with the blunt end of a shovel," M.J. laughed. "The outhouse was the coolest place around on that summer day, and he didn't want to give it up."

A slow patter of rain began to fall. We rolled up the truck windows and fell in behind a slow-moving stock truck that was making its way toward the interstate. On the back of the truck's doors, painted in black, were some words, but I couldn't read them through the mud-streaked windshield. M.J.'s wipers only worked at super-low speed, and mostly all they did was smear the dirt around.

M.J. and I leaned forward and squinted at the same time. She put on the gas and pulled up close behind the truck.

"Cluck, Cluck, Chicken Truck," it read.

We burst into laughter. M.J. looked at me sideways and nearly choked. "That ranks right up there with the Pickles Gap Grease and Grill!"

"The what?" I gasped between giggles.

"You heard me. You can have your oil changed while you eat lunch."

We laughed even more, so hard that M.J. had to dab at her eyes with a tissue.

Just as I was catching my breath, M.J.'s truck clanked and sputtered. M.J. sat up, instantly alert, but there was nothing she could do to keep the engine from dying. The truck rolled to a stop in a dip in the road.

"Rats," M.J. said. "She's overheated. Have to let her cool off for a few minutes."

"Overheated?" I asked. "But it's raining."

"Doesn't matter to this truck." M.J. rolled down the window, cocked her head outside, and looked at the sky. When she brought her head back in, her hair was sprinkled with raindrops and her expression had changed. She gripped the steering wheel tightly.

"What's the matter?" I asked.

She tried to smile. "We'll be OK here, provided it doesn't rain any harder."

I turned sideways and faced her. "Why? What would happen if it rained harder?"

M.J. pointed to either side of the truck. "We're sitting in a wash. When it rains, a six-foot wall of water can rush through here and sweep away anything or anybody in its path." She shot me a serious look. "Always stay out of washes when it rains."

I looked outside. The rain was slowing down.

"I'm serious about washes," M.J. said.

I shrugged. "I'm only going to be here a short time anyway, you know."

M.J. raised one eyebrow. "That so?"

Then I told her all of it. As we sat in the wash, waiting for the truck to cool off, I told her about the day of the alpacas' arrival, about how we couldn't get near them, and how Dad didn't even know he had bought a pregnant alpaca. "We'll be gone before school starts," I finished.

M.J. rubbed her chin. "Don't be so sure. After all, 'it is difficulties that show what men are made of.'" She flashed her eyes. "A Greek philosopher, name of Epictetus."

Eventually M.J. got the truck running again, and we went on making the rounds of general stores and ranches. The sun was sinking away by the time we finally turned up M.J.'s drive. After the long journey, she looked tired. We had covered almost every road in the county and picked up wood from four different places. All these people had saved wood for M.J., just to give it to her for nothing. I arched my back against the seat and sighed.

City people would never bother with this kind of thing.

[7]

the
escape

The next morning, after I had finished my chores, I left the barn and walked through the pasture without even bothering to look at the alpacas. After three weeks of serious effort on everyone's part except my own, the animals still acted as if they hated our guts.

Mom, Dad, and Angela couldn't seem to accept the facts. Despite the alpacas' treating us like we were infected aliens or something, my family thought we should name the beasts. Until then, we had been calling only a few of them by name. We'd already labeled, for obvious reasons, the Spitter and the Kicker, and Angela had dubbed the darkest one Chocolate.

"We should name the pregnant one next," Mom suggested as we stacked bales of hay inside the barn. She pointed to the fawn-colored female who was growing fatter every day. "I've already thought of a good name for her."

Angela waited as if this were the biggest announcement in the world.

Mom smiled. "She's kind of orangeish-tan, so how about Ginger?"

"OK," Angela said. "Let's name the rest according to color, too. You see those two white ones?" Angela pointed out two young females.

Mom smiled and nodded.

Angela continued, "We could call them Sugar and Frosty."

"I like that," Mom said. "What about the other two white ones, the males?"

Angela pursed her lips together. "How about Snowball and Cotton?"

How original. "The alpacas are not pets," I reminded them, sneering.

Mom put her hands on her hips and searched for something to say. "Laney, they just feel threatened. They're new here."

I glanced over at the herd and raised my eyebrows. The alpacas were huddling together against the shady side of the barn, so close to each other that they looked like one animal with numerous heads.

"Everything threatens them. I've never seen a nastier group of creatures," I countered. "Spitting and kicking and stomping." I lifted a bale of hay up onto the stack.

"They're just scared," Dad said.

I turned to him. "You want to name them, too?"

Dad shrugged. "I don't see why not."

It wasn't fair. Three against one, as always. I shoved another bale onto the stack. "They hate this place even more than I do."

Everyone went silent. Finally Dad said, "Laney, we understand that you miss Florida—"

I cut him off. "You don't understand at all!"

Mom sighed. "Honey, we all miss Florida a little. Probably not as much as you do, but this is our home now. Please give it a try here. Things will get better. I promise."

I wanted to scream. Instead I muttered through clenched teeth, "Things will not get better."

★

Early the next morning, everything came apart.

Mom got up from the breakfast table to pour herself a second cup of coffee and then went outside to get the paper. Every Thursday some guy in a pickup truck had been throwing a two-section newspaper, rolled up in a rubber band, into the sage and weeds in front of our house.

After a few minutes, Mom still hadn't returned. I figured she was searching among the thorns for the paper. But suddenly she came running back into the house, clutching her chest instead of a newspaper. She was having a hard time breathing. "Some of the fence is down," she gasped. "Counted the alpacas," she went on. "Only seventeen."

Dad sprang up and charged out of the house, with Mom close behind. Angela and I followed them out to the pasture, still in our nightgowns and slippers. Huge curlers hung out of Angela's hair, and I had a mouthful of cinnamon toast.

"We'll never be able to find them. They could be anywhere!" Mom whimpered.

"OK, OK—calm down. Hysterics aren't going to help," Dad said, shielding his eyes from the sun and scanning the surrounding land. We looked around too, but there was no sign of the three alpacas.

"I'm not hysterical!" Mom shrieked. "I'm merely concerned."

"Start working on the fence," Dad commanded Angela and me, ignoring Mom. "We don't want any more of them to get away."

In her bear-paw slippers, Angela took off to find some tools. I straightened my daisy-print nightgown and felt relief that hardly anyone ever traveled down our road. Then I ran over to the section of downed fencing to guard the opening.

Dad rolled up his shirtsleeves and paced in the dirt. Finally he said to Mom, "You stay here."

"But I can help you look for them," Mom said.

"No, I think I'm better off alone. Less of a threat to them."

"Well, which way do you suppose they went?" Mom asked.

He almost laughed. "I don't know."

Mom stood very still, her eyes filling with tears.

Dad gathered some rope and took off to look for tracks. Mom, her face looking pale, retreated back to the house.

"So what should we do?" Angela asked me when she returned with the toolbox.

"How would I know?" I scowled. "Try to put the fence back up, I guess."

Angela dropped the toolbox in a puff of dust. "Well, let's get dressed first. You guard the alpacas while I go in and change. Then we can trade places."

She disappeared inside. For a moment I thought about just walking away and letting all the alpacas escape. Those stupid animals—they had to be the dumbest creatures that ever stomped their feet on the face of this earth.

"Come on!" I screamed toward the house, starting to worry that any minute somebody actually would drive by and see me in my nightgown.

At last Angela appeared, and I ran inside to change.

As soon as I returned, we got to work. Angela set the first post back into its hole. When she did, I could see what the problem was. The holes Dad had dug weren't deep enough, and this soil was so dry and dusty it couldn't support the weight of the posts. All our efforts at piling dirt and stones around the bases had done no good. The alpacas only had to push a little and the fence posts would wiggle loose.

"It's the ground," I said as Angela shoveled dirt around the base of the post.

Angela rolled her eyeballs. "Well, we can't exactly change the ground, can we?"

I smiled. Today's events had gotten even to her. Her enthusiasm was evaporating as fast as the water in the alpacas' drinking trough.

When Angela was tired of shoveling, we switched places. She took a turn holding up the posts while I shoveled. We kept trading places like that, while the morning sun rose high in the sky. The whole time, the remaining alpacas huddled in a faraway corner of the pasture.

As soon as Angela and I had finished the fence,

we went inside and gulped down so much water we burped.

"Maybe the posts need to be set in something stronger, like concrete," I said.

"That's great. Another big job to do."

Finally Mom showed her face. Cheeks blotched with red and eyelids puffy, she looked as if she had been crying for hours. "I'll feed the alpacas," she said before she slipped outside.

By eleven o'clock, Dad still had not returned. Angela and I took turns going outside and staring out in all directions, but we could see no sign of him or the missing alpacas. Mom paced the floor.

Just when she had decided to take the car and go looking for him, he finally appeared north of the pasture, coming out of the dust. He had rounded up the three runaways and was herding them back, clapping his hands and weaving along several feet behind them.

Covered with dirt and streaked with sweat, Dad looked nothing like the distinguished man he had once been. At the gate, he left the alpacas and walked straight into the house without speaking to any of us. Mom followed him.

Angela and I had to get the three escapees back inside the gate on our own. And one of them I recognized immediately. The Spitter.

Angela immediately took charge of the situation. First she spoke loudly to the alpacas in an authoritative voice. When that didn't work, she waved sticks in the air and stomped her feet. I tried yelling at them too, but they only stared at me as if they couldn't figure out what my problem was.

The Spitter kicked at the ground and clucked and snorted. But he didn't spit or attack or attempt to run again. He just refused to go inside the pasture. So did the other two. It was a standoff. The alpacas stared. Angela and I stood and fumed. Finally, just when we had decided to give up and go inside for help, the alpacas sniffed the air, looked around with jerky glances, and crossed back into the enclosure on their own.

That evening Dad worked outside for hours to stabilize the fence. While Angela and I searched for rocks, he used the posthole digger to sink the posts deeper into the ground. Then, around their bases, he piled up the largest rocks we had found.

Meanwhile, Mom served a late dinner of roasted chicken. Dad wouldn't even come in to eat, but Angela and I, ravenous from working so hard, raced indoors and tore into the chicken—only to find it was still practically raw. Halfway to the bone, it oozed pink fluid. Mom threw down her napkin. Her eyes filled with tears again.

"Thanks for trying, Mom." I said it as gently as I could.

The skin around her mouth began to quiver. "Thank your *dad* for putting all our money into a herd of animals that hate us." She flew from her chair and ran back down the hall to her bedroom.

Angela looked up and shrugged. She shoved her chair back, stood up, and started searching the pantry for something else to eat. I put the chicken back in the oven, but I was too hungry to wait for it to finish cooking. I gulped down a can of tuna, two bananas, and almost a half gallon of milk.

Dad finally came in at dusk and collapsed in the recliner. He fell asleep almost immediately, without eating dinner or even taking a drink of water. I stood over him for a few minutes, watching.

"He's tired," Angela whispered from over my shoulder. "But he'll be OK."

Dad smelled like a mixture of sweat and dirt. He used to smell of Aramis, Mom's favorite cologne. He used to dress for success. Now, his jeans and western shirt were faded and stained, and his boots were scuffed and dust-covered. His hair was plastered against his forehead, and his fingernails were black around the edges.

And he had never fallen asleep in a chair before.

Angela and I stared a while longer. After a few

minutes, Dad's mouth fell open. Deep snoring sounds emerged from his throat. Underneath his lids, his eyeballs jerked rapidly from side to side.

I glanced at Angela.

"He's dreaming," she whispered. Then she tiptoed away, leaving me there to stare on my own.

I thought of all Dad's "It Used to Be" stories and remembered all the dreams he'd shared with us. Surely, this was not what he'd had in mind.

Oh well. No one would listen to me before. Now they were finding out the hard way that I was right. But as hard as I tried, I could no longer summon up my anger. For the first time, I actually felt a bit sorry for my parents.

★

The next morning, after I had finished my chores, I headed over to M.J.'s. Along the way I spotted another dead deer beside the road. This one was a young buck with a brand-new set of antlers. They were incredible. Covered with deep brown, soft-looking fuzz, they grew out of the top of his head like twisted tree limbs.

A strong urge to touch the soft velvet of those antlers came over me. I reached down and brushed my fingertips along one antler. It felt like suede.

"Can't anything be done?" I asked M.J. later.

"I wish." M.J. took a sip of sun tea. "Now come to think of it, I did see something once . . . Where would that be now?" She got up from the dinette and started looking around her tiny living room. I turned sideways and tucked my feet under my legs. When M.J. had an idea, she was fun to watch.

She wobbled from one stack of books and magazines to another, searching through the piles. M.J. had a system of organizing her stuff that no other person on earth could ever figure out.

"Here," she said as she straightened up. A smile spread over her face. "Here it is."

She pulled out a catalogue so old it had no corners left. She flipped through it until she found the page she was looking for. "They're whistles that go on the front of cars," she said, pointing to the page. "They emit a high-pitched sound that scares the deer off the road."

She showed me the ad for the deer whistles. They were about four inches high and made of metal. They could be mounted on the front hood or bumper of a car. The ad said that the sound they made couldn't be heard by humans, only animals, and that they were an effective way to save the lives of wild animals and avoid damage to your vehicle.

"You've given me an idea." M.J. slid herself back into the seat. "This is a wholesale catalogue.

We could buy a bunch of these for real cheap and then sell them to people."

I perked up. "Really?"

M.J. shot me a stern look and shook her index finger in the air. "Now, I don't normally deal in anything that's not recyclable or made with recycled materials. But for this, I'll make an exception."

"It's for a good cause."

"Yes," M.J. said, studying me again. "Yes, and maybe good for you, too." She closed the catalogue and handed it over. "You'll have to call on your phone to see if they're still available. Find out how much they cost now."

I took the catalogue, my head swimming with questions. How would we sell these deer whistles? Would the people around here really buy them?

Before I could speak, however, M.J. said, "There's a saying, Laney: 'To have a grievance is to have a purpose in life.'"

[8]

humming

As soon as I got home, I took the cordless phone inside the bathroom and called the company that sold the deer whistles. But my heart fell when the customer service representative told me that the prices had almost doubled over the years since that catalogue had come out. The minimum order was sixty and would cost nearly two hundred dollars. I had some money I'd saved from babysitting back in Florida, but not nearly enough. And M.J. certainly didn't have the money.

I marched outside to Dad. "I need to earn some money. If I did extra chores, would you pay me?"

Dad stopped mucking out the barn and put a

gloved hand on his hip. "You want me to give you more chores?"

"As many as I can get."

He looked puzzled.

"More chores?" he asked again.

I nodded.

Dad tried not to let me see him smile. "Of course I can give you more to do. But what's this all about?"

I stared out at the pasture, at Dad's precious alpacas. How could I explain to him why I cared more about common deer than his animals? "What difference does it make? Just let me know what I can do to earn some money."

Now he really looked curious. He leaned the shovel against the barn. "I'd really like to know what you need all this money for. It's not like there are a lot of shopping places around here."

I sighed. He wasn't going to let up. "It's for deer whistles. To save deer on the roads around here."

"Deer whistles?" He frowned. "I don't get it."

"No, you wouldn't."

"Try me."

I chewed my lip. "Deer get hit by cars all the time around here. And M.J. and I found some special whistles in a catalogue. They can save lives and prevent accidents. We want to buy a bunch of them to sell to people. OK?"

Dad stared at me for a long time, as if he didn't know what to say. But eventually he just shrugged and said, "OK."

By the next morning, he had thought of something for me to do. He strolled up to me as I was cleaning the water trough. "Have you noticed that the alpacas always leave their droppings in that far corner of the field?" he said.

Something gross was coming my way, I knew it. But I answered as nicely as I could. "No."

"That is one of the many advantages of this animal." My dad the alpaca expert had returned. "They are very easy to clean up after. And did you know that one of the best fertilizers for growing flowers, fruits, and vegetables is alpaca dung?"

Dung? I felt my stomach doing somersaults.

"That can be an extra job for you. You can collect the droppings."

I wanted to wail out loud. But instead I made myself nod OK, because I needed the money.

So after I had finished all of my regular chores, I started shoveling up alpaca dung. I wore dirty clothes and two pairs of gloves, and I'd swear it had to be the hottest day of the entire summer.

Flies buzzed and looped around me, and the air reeked. I shoveled the dung into a large pile while, off to the side, the alpacas snorted and stared at me and dug at the ground with their toenails.

Finally, when I had all the dung in one big heap, I grabbed some burlap bags out of the barn and brought them back to the pile. I stood still for a few moments. How was I going to get this stuff inside the bags? I really needed someone to help me hold the bag open, but Angela was already finished with her work for the day and had gone inside to help Mom make lunch. Dad was nowhere to be seen.

I decided I could manage on my own. I plunged the shovel into the dung and lifted the first big mound of dung balls into the air. I kicked open the burlap bag and shoved the dung in. It almost worked. I got most of the dung inside the bag. Then I let myself breathe out. It would be easier from now on, as the bag got fuller.

Two shovelfuls later, I thought I saw something out of the corner of my eye. I turned to look. Two of the alpacas, Chocolate and the Kicker, were brushing up against the fence, as if they were deliberately trying to knock it down.

"Hey," I shouted at them. "Get away from there!"

They lifted their heads in my direction and sniffed the air. Then they went right back to what they were doing.

"Stop it!" I yelled, turning toward them. I lost my

balance and stumbled forward, stepping right into the middle of all the alpaca dung. I was in up to my ankles, right through the outer crust of the dung balls and into the smelly mush inside.

I threw down the shovel and stepped out of the pile. I stomped around on the dirt and grass and tried to shake the mushy stuff off my shoes. But it was hopeless. My cross-trainers were covered.

Hot tears began to build up behind my eyelids. How could anything be grosser than this? This horrible place. These horrible animals. I swallowed several times even though my throat was dry. My eyes burned and filled, but I was determined to keep the tears back.

It didn't work. As I ran into the barn and began swiping my shoes on the straw that I had just spread that morning, the tears spilled out and poured down my face.

It wasn't fair. There I was, working hard and trying to do the right thing, trying to keep the alpacas from knocking over the fence again. And look where it got me—covered in their stinky slime.

I should have just let the stupid animals escape. Let them disappear into the dust, never to be seen again. Or let them do something so awful that Mom and Dad would decide to sell them along with this miserable ranch and take us back to Florida.

It could still happen. After all, the next day the vet was coming to immunize the alpacas. I couldn't wait to see what would happen when the vet tried to stick needles through the hides of these brats. This could be the day my parents decided to leave.

★

Early in the morning, I bounced out of bed like a clown popping out of a jack-in-the-box. When the vet arrived, he sat down with Dad at the kitchen table to go over the procedure. "Never seen one of these animals before," the vet said. "But I studied up before I drove over."

Well, what a shot of confidence that was. I could barely keep from laughing out loud.

First, the vet drew up the vaccinations, capped the syringes, and dropped them into his front shirt pockets. Then he told the rest of us the plan, which was really quite simple—and doomed, in my opinion. He would try to ease up to the animals, one by one, and give them their shots. The rest of us were supposed to stand close by to assist if needed. "I've learned a few things from working with nervous animals over the years. Don't make direct eye contact with them," he warned us. "It can be viewed as a threat."

I smelled disaster coming.

Silently, we slipped through the gate. One at a time we crept up to the herd, making sure not to look at any of the alpacas directly. We got as close to them as we could. Then the vet approached one of the white females, the one Angela called Sugar.

He made such smooth, easy movements that he could have been a tree swaying in the breeze. He let Sugar sniff at his hand and then he gently laid a palm on her withers.

My heart sank. This might not be so hard after all. I was sure that at the touch of a human, the alpaca would rear back and spit. Instead, Sugar sniffed up the vet's arm and behaved herself. While he reached into his pocket for a syringe, my parents, Angela, and I stood still and barely breathed.

An evil thought sprang into my mind. And once it had planted itself there, I simply couldn't stop myself. As the vet injected Sugar, I looked right into her eyes. And not only did I look, but I shot daggers at her. I challenged her with my glare—*bolt, kick, spit, do something, you idiot!*

But Sugar simply tilted her head to one side and gazed back at me. Her little mouth seemed to curl up on both sides, and if I didn't know it was impossible, I would have sworn that Sugar was smiling.

I fumed inside. Just when I wanted them to mis-behave, they suddenly had to go and act like angels.

Maybe they could sense that they were no longer in the hands of amateurs, or maybe they were just sick of resisting us. I don't know, but for some reason they let the vet move among them and give them all their immunizations without any trouble. A few of the males looked him over and made some clicking noises, but they didn't do anything else no matter how hard I tried to aggravate them with my eyes. Even the Spitter let me down.

And that's not all. Before he left, the vet confirmed that Ginger was definitely pregnant, and far along, too. For the rest of the day I was so beaten down I couldn't even look up at the sky.

Over dinner that night, Mom worked on a new shopping list. Every few minutes I could hear her let out a long sigh. Finally she looked up at me. "Tomorrow we're going shopping in Carsonville. The alpacas went through a lot today, getting their shots, so we're going to leave them alone for a bit."

I perked up. "We're not feeding them?" It was a sick joke, I knew. But I couldn't resist.

Mom looked teary. "Of course we'll feed them. We're just not going to, to . . ." She paused, searching for the right word.

"Try to make them our pets anymore," I finished for her.

"Right," Mom said. "The vet advises that we

approach them when necessary but otherwise keep our distance."

Good, I thought. *They're finally starting to give up.*

But as I ate Mom's cooking, which had actually started to improve, I found it hard to get the food to slide down my throat. Even the ice cream we had for dessert didn't taste nearly as sweet as usual. I kept remembering how badly Mom and Dad had wanted to make friends with the alpacas.

After dinner Dad paid me my regular allowance plus the additional money I had earned doing extra chores for the past two days. Maybe now, I thought, I would have the two hundred dollars I needed to order the whistles. I ran to my room and fished out all the coins and dollar bills I had stuffed under my mattress. I spread them out on the floor. Then I pulled out the money Dad had just paid me and added it to the pile. I counted it hopefully. But when I picked up the very last coin, my shoulders sank. Not nearly enough.

I pushed the curls off my face and felt the tears build up behind my eyelids again. I would simply have to do more chores, more horrible chores. Slowly I lined up the dollar bills side by side and smoothed them out flat. Then I stacked the coins into columns. As I worked, I studied my knuckles. They were so reddened and callused that I hardly recognized them anymore. I crawled into bed and closed my eyes, trying to shut out the whole horrendous day.

★

In the middle of the night, I awoke.

Maybe the day's events were still haunting me. Or maybe it was the full moon hanging in the frame of my window, sending powdery beams of light into the room and casting shadows across the floor.

A few trapped insects buzzed against the screen, and I could hear crickets chirping outside. Too many thoughts and visions gnawed at me. The dead deer and not enough money for the deer whistles. Alpaca dung all over my feet. Even my parents' giving up on getting friendly with the alpacas didn't make me feel as good as I thought it would.

I rolled over and punched my pillow.

I sighed and closed my eyes. Finally I began to drift away. But when I arrived at that in-between state, no longer awake but not really sleeping either, I heard a new noise. A hum.

My eyes flew open. I lay perfectly still and listened hard. No, this was definitely not crickets.

I slipped out of bed. I found my robe and stuck my feet into my shoes. I crept down the hallway and slipped quietly out the front door. The light of the full moon lit my way. Louder now, the humming continued. I followed the sound around to the back of the house, to the pasture.

It was the alpacas.

In the center of the pasture they stood calm and motionless. Their small, pointed ears perked high in the air, and their heads tilted in the direction of the moon. And they were making a sound like nothing I'd ever heard before. It was sort of a purr, like the sound Claws made when he licked himself, only this was louder and deeper. And at the same time it was sort of a rumble, like the sound of distant thunder, only gentler.

I stood there, frozen. I stared and listened, stared and listened. I'm not sure how much time went by.

What could it mean? Why were they doing it? Did the humming mean the alpacas were happy? Or did it mean something was wrong? Were they trying to communicate with each other, or with me?

And what was I supposed to do about it? Maybe I should have paid better attention when Dad read out of the alpaca book. Surely it would have mentioned this humming. I glanced toward the house and wondered if I should wake my parents.

No, I wouldn't tell anybody. Better to keep it to myself. If I told my family, they would probably all come creeping outside every night hoping to hear it, losing needed sleep and bothering the alpacas. And who knew if the alpacas would ever hum again anyway? Besides, nothing seemed to be wrong with the animals.

I returned to bed.

But every time I closed my eyes that night and every night after, the sound returned to me—that deep, soft murmuring.

I wanted to see if I could imitate the sound, but I was afraid someone might hear me. So I did it in the shower, when the sound of running water drowned out my voice. I tried to imitate the low rumbling tone, but I never could match the real sound, the sound of a herd of alpacas humming.

[9]

the pull
of the earth

The veterinarian's visit turned out to be the best thing that could have happened. Even though I wanted to strangle the alpacas for not acting up, at least they had gotten their immunizations, and Mom and Dad had finally given up on treating them like pets.

Now everything was pretty quiet around our place. We simply did our chores and left the alpacas alone. Every so often we drove out to the Kmart in Carsonville.

I kept doing extra jobs, earning extra money. I helped Mom and Dad repair the roof of the house and weatherproof the storage shed. I helped build more shelves inside the barn. Then I raked up all the big rocks and clods of dirt from the pasture.

After a long day of hard work, I would walk down to M.J.'s place to tell her how much money I had earned. Every day I was getting closer to buying those deer whistles.

Altogether, I had to admit that things around our place were better, calmer.

Except for the nights. Almost every night now, the alpacas' humming woke me out of a sound sleep. I was sure it was getting louder, and yet no one else seemed to hear it. Not even Mom, who used to sleep so lightly she could hear Claws scratching her furniture in the middle of the night.

The alpacas would always start humming as soon as the moon rose. Just as its light began streaming through my open window, I would wake up to the sound of that low, rolling tone. Usually I just lay there, listening to the strange sound and begging for the alpacas to stop it so I could get some rest.

But it didn't work. They just kept humming, as if they couldn't help themselves.

One night I had heard enough. I crept outside in my nightgown and walked to the pasture. I took one step up onto the bottom rung of the gate and let my arms dangle over the top.

I watched the herd huddle together and lift their

ears to the sky, making that indescribable sound. I listened for what seemed like an eternity. Then I noticed one of the alpacas slowly making her way over toward me.

I didn't move. I didn't look directly at her. I kept my eyes away, just as the vet had told us to. But I could see her out of the corner of my eye. She kept on coming, right up to the fence where I stood.

It was Ginger, pregnant Ginger. Still holding myself as silently as I could, I felt her moist nose brush up against my arm. She blew warm spurts of air as she sniffed up and down, first one of my arms and then the other.

I decided to take a chance. Slowly I turned my hand over. Ginger sniffed my palm and half-curled fingers. Then she let me touch the bridge of her nose. The corners of her mouth seemed to turn upward into a smile.

I moved my hand up to the dense patch of wool on top of Ginger's head.

Then I remembered something.

When Angela and I were little, we used to climb up into the attic, our favorite place to play house. We had an old, ripped armchair stored up there, and we would pull wads of stuffing out of it and blow the tufts high in the air. Then we would watch them fall back down to the floor like feathers.

Ginger was soft, just like the stuffing that came out of that old armchair.

I pulled my hand back.

What was I doing? Everyone else wanted contact with these animals, not me. I didn't even like them.

I decided to look Ginger right in the eye to scare her away, but when I turned in her direction, I couldn't show her anything mean. At that moment, everything inside of me seemed to settle out like a smooth sea.

And Ginger just kept on standing there with me by the fence, as if she would have let me touch her all night long. By the light of the moon, I could see her large, round eyes shining, looking straight at me, filled with something I'd swear looked a little like sadness.

Then it occurred to me. Maybe Ginger was homesick. Homesick for the mountains of Peru, even if she'd never even seen them.

Quickly I pushed myself away from the fence and swallowed hard. Maybe the alpacas were longing for their true homeland as much as I was missing Florida. It was hard to be away from where you belonged. But they were still the reason I got stuck out here. I took a step backward and made myself turn around and walk back toward the house.

No one could ever know that this had happened.

If my parents or Angela found out I had touched Ginger, they would probably think that I had some special "bond" with her, that I had a way with the alpacas or something. And I certainly did not.

★

The next day, while M.J. and I worked together in her flower beds, I tried to push all thoughts of the alpacas far, far away. I was silent as I dug. Every so often I could feel M.J. shooting glances over in my direction.

"There's nothing like working the earth with your hands," she said as she dragged her fingers through the dirt, separating the soil around a clump of purple daisies. She pressed and patted down the earth around a new seedling.

I said, "I'm more of a water person myself."

M.J. kept working. "The ocean, yes." She stole another glance at me. "It's lovely. But for me, there's nothing like solid ground under my feet. The pull of the earth, Laney. It's special, too."

I shrugged. Not for me. I belonged by the ocean. The sea could change and surprise me every day. The solid earth was boring.

"Time to plant pansies," M.J. said, pushing some seedlings in small plastic containers toward me and then passing me a trowel. "Here, you need this."

I took the shovel, dug a hole in the dirt, and then reached for the seedlings.

"Careful with the roots," M.J. said. "You'll have to set them in with your hands."

I gently placed the plant in its hole, then I pushed the soil around the roots and patted it snugly with my palms.

"Beautiful," M.J. said after we had finished. She sat back on her knees and admired our work. "In the spring, the tulips will come up in this bed. They're my favorites. Can't wait for you to see them."

"I won't see them." I glanced at M.J. out of the corner of my eye. "We'll be long gone by then."

M.J. picked a small sprig of parsley from the garden and tasted it. She scowled as she chewed. "Bitter, bitter."

I knew she meant me, too. "You don't understand," I told her. Then I let out a long breath. "I hate it here. I've been working so hard and I'm tired."

"Hard work is good for a body," M.J. huffed as she struggled to her feet. She handed me the remaining seedlings. "Here, put these in the greenhouse."

I pushed myself to my feet. "I've been doing as many chores as I possibly can, and I still don't have enough money for the whistles."

M.J. slowly rocked herself toward the trailer. "Follow me."

Inside, she opened the bottom drawer of her kitchen cabinet. "Let's see," she murmured softly as she plucked out an old purse. "I have a little put away for a rainy day."

She dug through the purse. "I'll round out what you need moneywise." She pulled out a roll of bills held together with a rubber band.

"No, M.J., you can't," I said, knowing that it was probably all the extra money she had.

"Sure I can. Got to have those whistles before the county fair in August," she said. "We can sell a lot of them there."

"Are you sure?"

"Sure I'm sure." She handed me the money. "Well, I'm going back to work now. You can take a rest if you like, but I've got a lot of birdhouses to build before the fair." She wobbled out the door.

I didn't count the money until after M.J. had gone outside. Then, in my head, I added it to my own savings and figured out how much we had altogether. When I had finished, I pressed the money close to my chest. Finally there was enough. I could order the whistles the next day.

I went outside to tell M.J. She was in her shed, hard at work. She had selected a piece of wood and was measuring and marking it with a pencil. Then she cut the wood with a handsaw and sanded over the rough spots. Finally, she nailed the pieces together, hammering with a determination that amazed me. What M.J. lacked in her spine she made up with her hands. She was strong.

"This is one of my two designs," M.J. said when she had completed a birdhouse. "I call this one the Gold Mine." She turned it around to face me. Tall and narrow with a pointed roof, it looked like a picture I'd once seen of an old mining shack hanging off a cliff face. She handed it to me. "Here, it's for you," she said as she dusted off her hands.

I shook my head. "No, thanks. I mean, not that I don't want it, but you need to sell it at the fair."

M.J. scoffed. "I'll make plenty more."

I looked down at my birdhouse. A knothole stared back at me, a knothole M.J. had placed on the front on purpose. "It gives them character," she explained. "Everyone wants one with a knothole. They sell first."

I frowned. "Why do they sell first? I mean, isn't a knothole a flaw in the wood?"

M.J. thought that one over. "Well, I guess you could say that."

"I remember when we put up our wood fence in Florida. My dad didn't want any knotholes in it."

"Ah, but this is different." M.J. took off her apron and hung it on a nail. "Wood for fencing is supposed to be pretty much the same. You know, so the slats of wood all look identical when they're lined up next to each other." She smiled and raised her eyebrows. "But birdhouses aren't the same as fences."

I frowned again.

"Think about it, Laney. Is every shell in the ocean the same? The knotholes are what make each birdhouse special. Each one is different, just like the person who buys it."

All the way home, I thought about the off-the-wall things M.J. was always saying. I carried my birdhouse in a paper bag with handles, swinging it silently back and forth.

And I tried to do as M.J. had said, to discover the pull of the earth, to understand what she found so special in this landlocked place. I tried not to think about floating over waves and the feel of wet sand between my toes. I tried, but the pull of the ocean kept stealing me away.

As I approached our house, I stopped dead in my tracks. What in the world was going on?

Everyone was out in the pasture instead of inside getting ready for dinner. Near the gate, Dad was walking with one of the alpacas, slowly leading the animal around on a halter. It was one of the rose-gray females, Pansy, and she was allowing herself to be led without showing any resistance at all. In fact, she held her head high and walked lightly, as if she was proud of herself.

And Dad. He could barely contain his joy. He looked up and crooked a finger at me, signaling me to come and see, but I couldn't move.

Mom and Angela hung on the gate, watching. A few minutes later, they took turns leading Pansy. Angela strutted proudly as she took the halter in her hands. Mom's face beamed in the fading daylight. She looked so beautiful.

For a second I almost felt happy for them. Then I remembered.

This wasn't supposed to be happening.

I ran to my room. I stretched out on my bed and started counting the little bumps on the ceiling. I sat back up and looked around for something to do.

On the floor I saw the bag holding my birdhouse. I reached down and pulled it out the bag. Then I set it on top of one of my unpacked boxes. I touched it with my fingertips and noticed dirt underneath my fingernails, dirt instead of sand. Ignoring the dirt, I started filling out the deer-whistle order form that M.J. had given me. I'd get a check from Dad later, in return for all my cash, and in the morning I'd put the order in the mail. While the rest of my family were getting all chummy with the alpacas, I'd be doing something that really mattered.

[10]

Leotie

One morning about two weeks later, Mom, Dad, Angela, and I got up early and drove all the way to the interstate, just to eat breakfast at the Big L Truck Stop. I played oldies on the jukebox and watched all sorts of interesting characters stream in and out of the restaurant. We listened to the talk of the truck drivers and the waitresses, while the odors of diesel fuel, hot rubber, and fried foods drifted in the air.

When we returned, there was a brown box sitting on the front porch. My heart jumped into my throat. It had to be the deer whistles. I carried the box to my room, tore at the tape, and folded open the top flaps.

Inside, packed in foam popcorn, were the deer whistles. Each one came with a folded sheet of instructions showing how to mount the whistle on your car or truck. I picked up a whistle and rolled it in my hand, smiling. M.J. had said we needed these in time for the county fair, and they'd arrived with over a week to spare. I couldn't wait to tell her.

A little while later, as I was stuffing some whistles into a bag to take down to M.J.'s, I heard rushed footsteps in the hallway and the squeak of the screen door opening and closing over and over again. I flew to my window to see what was going on. Maybe another escape?

But all seemed pretty quiet out in the pasture. So I went to my doorway. "What's going on?" I asked Mom as she passed by, heading down the hall.

"It's time," Mom said.

I stood still for a few moments, letting it sink in. Ginger was giving birth. The vet had come by once more and told us what he had witnessed with llama births. He had scratched his head and run his hands along Ginger's sides. "Any day now. That's my best opinion." Then he had driven off in a brown cloud and left us to handle the situation on our own.

Poor Ginger. She had grown so large she could barely waddle around the corral. And now she was in the hands of amateurs.

I remained frozen in my doorway. Dad had told me, "When the time comes, you don't have to help."

But now that the time had arrived, I felt torn. Once, a long time ago, my friend and I had stayed up half the night waiting for her very pregnant dog to give birth. But we had fallen asleep shortly after midnight, and in the morning, that dog had seven newborn puppies coiled up against her side.

I jumped into my shoes. This opportunity I didn't want to miss. I flew outside and ran to the barn without even tying my shoelaces.

Ginger stood over a pile of fresh straw that Dad had spread in the quietest, darkest corner of the barn. As I drew closer, Ginger turned her head and looked up at me. She appeared surprisingly normal. Her eyes were the same—large, black spheres that seemed to bulge from their sockets. The corners of her mouth curled up in that same plucky smile she had shown me the night in the pasture.

I couldn't help myself. I smiled back. Then I turned to Dad. "How do you know it's time?"

Dad shook his head. "I'm not positive, but she's been acting strange, sitting and standing and rolling on the ground as if she's uncomfortable."

"We brought her into the barn, just in case," Mom added.

Angela and Dad stroked Ginger's neck. I stood by

her side. Mom checked her camera to make certain it was loaded with film, and then she set the camera down on a bale of hay.

Inside the barn, the air was so still that each one of Ginger's breaths came out in loud puffs. Outside, the afternoon wind picked up and was blowing in gusts. Ginger began to lift her tail and strain and push from deep within her body.

"Come on, girl, you can do it," Dad whispered in her ear.

"Good girl," Angela said.

Ginger alternately stood, then stepped about, as if she couldn't find a comfortable position. At one point she gasped, and her eyes grew a little wild.

Just when Mom had decided we should call the vet, we heard something outside over the sound of the wind. It was the alpacas humming. Mom, Dad, and Angela looked at each other like, *What on earth is that?*

"It's OK," I whispered. "I've heard it before."

Suddenly Ginger stretched her neck and strained. She seemed to stop breathing for long moments, and her abdomen turned as hard as one of M.J.'s rocks. Then she lifted her tail, and water poured out.

"Her water just broke," Dad said with relief. "It shouldn't be long now."

Mom clasped her hands together and beamed.

Then we all stood perfectly still and waited.

But Ginger abruptly sat down in the straw. Dad looked alarmed. "This isn't right," he said. "She's supposed to remain standing. The birth can take too long this way."

Dad reached down and tried to urge Ginger back into a standing position, but she refused to budge.

"Look!" Angela cried out. From the birth canal, two tiny feet appeared.

Dad moved behind Ginger. "We need to help her get the cria out quickly. Hold her," he ordered me.

Quickly I knelt down in the straw and placed both of my hands on Ginger's withers. Dad took hold of the tiny slick feet and carefully pulled. He grimaced, and sweat began to pour from his forehead. My heart pounded up inside my throat.

Hurry, hurry, my mind screamed.

"It's coming," Dad said, nearly choking on his own words. He kept pulling while the front legs of the cria slowly emerged—two straight, skinny sticks that began to move on their own. When he let go of the feet and stood back, his forehead was glistening with sweat, and his face was as red as one of M.J.'s tomatoes. "Come on, girl," he said to Ginger. "We can't pull out the rest. You've got to do it yourself."

I sank my fingers into the soft wool on top of Ginger's head and gently stroked. When she looked my way, I stared directly into her eyes and pleaded silently with her. *You can do this,* I told her.

Ginger strained again, and a tiny nose appeared. Dad and I stood back and let Ginger push. Mom took a step closer to help, but Dad held out his hand and motioned her to stay back.

With a huge thrust of energy, Ginger pushed down, and the rest of the head emerged. The body and hind legs quickly followed. The little cria slipped out into the world and plopped into the soft straw, squirming. When I saw the newborn take gulps of air into its lungs, I realized I'd been holding my breath, too.

Dad laughed out loud. Angela clapped as if she had just seen the best performance of her life. Mom remembered her camera and started snapping pictures. Ginger began nosing her baby up and down.

I tasted fresh tears in the corners of my mouth. I struggled to find my voice. I wanted to greet this little creature properly, but I found my words had gotten lost somewhere deep inside my chest, and I could only stare without speaking.

"It's a girl!" Dad shouted. "Probably about fifteen pounds."

"She's perfect," Mom said.

Within minutes the cria struggled to stand. Rising on wobbly, fragile-looking legs, she wavered, then plunked to the ground. But an hour later, she was nursing and walking easily at Ginger's side. Her white coat had dried and plumped. Her dark eyes, black as a bunny's and lined with lashes, studied this strange new world.

My parents and Angela spent the rest of the day watching the cria, first in the barn and then later when she followed Ginger out to the pasture. In the fading sunlight, as I finished up my chores, I could see her out of the corner of my eye. She frolicked and kicked up her heels as if it felt so good to be alive and free of that small space inside her mother. She tested out her pencil-thin legs, running and jumping and pawing the dirt. She sniffed the air and examined everything around her.

Mom motioned me over to the gate where she, Dad, and Angela were standing. "What in the world was that sound we heard while Ginger was giving birth?"

"They hum," I told them flatly. "The alpacas hum together. I've heard them many times before." I shrugged. "I don't have a clue what it means, but almost every night they hum as a group, even louder when the moon is full."

"Amazing," Dad said. "I've been wondering when we would get to hear that." He looked so pleased. "Hey, I have an idea. Angela has named almost all of the other alpacas. I say it's your turn, Laney, to pick a name." He gestured toward the cria. "For her."

Everyone looked at me. I knew what they were thinking: if they could get me to name the baby, then maybe I would get attached to her and start liking it here.

"Yes, Laney," said my sister. "What should we name her?"

I gazed at the cria. She did deserve a name. And if I picked it, at least she would get a good one, not some stupid color like the others.

"Be right back," I said. I ran inside the house and dug into my box marked *Books*. I searched for my name book, pulled it out, sprawled out on the floor, and began going through the book page by page.

The name had to be perfect. The cria shouldn't suffer her whole life with the wrong name. I had to find the one name that would be perfect for her, just as *Merissa* would have been perfect for me. Maybe another ocean name, a water name.

But instead my eyes landed on *Leotie*, a Native American name meaning "flower of the prairie." It was beautiful. It sounded like something M.J. would come up with. And after all, the cria was born on the prairie.

I ran back outside, holding the book open to show my family the name.

"Leotie," Angela said. "Flower of the prairie."

"Is that what it means?" Mom asked. "Why, that's lovely."

Then I realized what was happening. I closed the book and swallowed hard.

How had I gotten so carried away? Somehow the excitement of the birth had swept me off course, made me lose sight of my goal. I wanted to be far away from these animals. I had no business naming one, not even this newborn.

I looked down at my sore hands and thought about them instead of the cria. I handed the book over to Angela. "Never mind. You pick one." I tore my eyes away from the cria and walked away.

★

Several nights later, while everyone else slept, the humming sound lured me outside once again. I climbed up onto the top railing of the gate and watched the moon light up the pasture in a silver glow. I followed the herd with my eyes until I could pick them out, mother and newborn.

Angela had decided the name *Leotie* was too complicated and was calling the cria Fluffy instead. But in the moonlight and to myself, I called the cria by her real name.

"Leotie," I whispered to her. "Leotie."

[11]

the
fair

I stayed away from the alpacas for the next several nights. Even though I could hear them humming outside, the entire herd rumbling together, I resisted. Instead I pushed the pillow down tightly over my head and tried to block out the sound.

But the night before the county fair, I found it impossible to sleep. I turned from side to side, trying to imagine what the next day would be like.

What if M.J. and I didn't sell any deer whistles?

What if Mom and Dad embarrassed me beyond belief? Several days before, my parents had come up with the idea of bringing one of the alpacas to the fair. They were incredibly proud of their progress with the animals, and they thought that the local people would surely want to see one of these unusual creatures. But I had my doubts. What would people really think? Would they find my family as amusing as Tim and his father had?

A sense of dread came over me. I couldn't stand to think about it anymore. I got out of bed and found myself walking outside.

As I neared the pasture, I looked up at the stars. Out here, away from the city lights, the stars were always spectacular—like a million sparkling shells floating on a black sea. But tonight they seemed even more dense and bright.

I walked to the gate and hung my arms over the railing. The herd grazed for a while and then stopped, lifted their heads, and began to hum. It came in swells, sometimes softer, sometimes louder, then softer again. And just as before, Ginger soon broke away from the herd and headed in my direction. At her heels came Leotie, already grown bigger but still looking like a bundle of white fuzz with stick legs and black buttons for eyes. I touched Ginger. I stroked the soft wool on the bridge of her nose and the patch on top of her head.

Then I searched the ground around me for some grass. The herd had long since chomped away what-ever grass had grown within the pasture. But outside the gate I could still find some soft patches. I pulled up a handful and dangled my arm over the gate.

I held the grass out to Ginger. She nibbled it right up. I had expected her lips to feel a little slobbery, but they were dry. They felt like fat fingers carefully reading my palm. After she finished, I turned away and searched for more grass. I pulled up another handful and, this time, crouched down near the ground, reaching my arm in between the bottom two rungs of the gate. Steadily Leotie moved over to me without any sign of fear. She nudged her nose against my arm and sniffed her way down to my palm. Then, nuzzling my hand, she investigated the grass. Still too young to eat it, she knocked most of it to the ground.

I could feel her warm breath and the tickling sensation of her small lips on my skin. I breathed in the air that surrounded her and caught the scent of warm milk and wool.

★

I woke up the next morning to the sound of Angela screaming. While she and Mom were getting ready to cook breakfast, Claws had slipped in through the door carrying a field mouse he had caught, still alive. Angela shrieked, and Claws had dropped the mouse on the kitchen floor. The tiny, terrified creature promptly scurried away over the scratched linoleum. Mom and Dad had to begin a search of the entire house. I got dressed and helped, but we never did find that mouse. We gave up when it was time to get ready for the fair.

Dad shrugged. "There are probably mice in the cellar anyway."

I carried the box of deer whistles to M.J.'s place and helped her load them and her birdhouses into the back of her pickup truck. We needed to get to the fairgrounds early to set up before the gates opened. But that old truck had different ideas. It chose this day, of all days, to refuse to start. M.J. worked for about twenty minutes to get the engine to turn over before she finally gave up.

I had to run back to our house and get Dad. He ended up having to drive us to the fairgrounds and then come back for Mom, Angela, and Pansy, the rose-gray alpaca he'd chosen to bring.

By the time M.J. and I finally got settled into our spot at the fair, I felt like we had already had enough excitement for one day.

We set up our booth, which was really just a folding table and lawn chairs, under a faded blue tarp. Over our heads M.J. hung a sign that said "Laney and the Birdhouse Lady." We arranged the birdhouses and whistles on the table.

Other vendors set up their booths and then sat at shaded tables or put the finishing touches on their displays.

At opening time, fairgoers began streaming in to browse and shop. I took a deep breath and waited for customers to come. M.J. and I had decided on just a slight markup for the deer whistles, about fifty cents apiece, so that the price wouldn't keep people from buying them.

As we waited, I started squirming in my seat. I wanted to see the rest of the fair. And, I had to admit, a part of me just wanted to get away from the booth. I couldn't help wondering what people were thinking of me when they saw me there with M.J. People liked her, I knew, but she was still the county weirdo. Would they think I was weird too? And what if they thought the deer whistles were stupid?

And of course M.J. had to bring along stacks of yellowed pamphlets on everything from soil conservation to solar energy. Every so often, out of the clear blue, M.J. would shout, "Recycle now! Save our planet!" I idly picked up one of the pamphlets and read it. *Recycling to Save the Earth.*

M.J. glanced over and winked at me. "Always like to hand them out at the fair. People would miss it if I didn't." She was wearing a cotton sundress and had combed her hair away from her face. I could swear she even had on a little bit of lipstick. Earlier, when I had gawked at her changed appearance, M.J. had explained: "The county fair is the biggest event of the summer. Everyone comes out, even people you don't see except once or twice a year."

Just then a man strode up to the booth and said, "Heard about them whistles." My first customer. He had the biggest eyebrows I had ever seen in my life. Sticking out like a pair of straw brooms, the hair must have been two inches long. I had to peel my eyes off of him and get serious.

I straightened up. "You mount them on your front bumper, and the sound scares the deer off the roads. They are very reasonably priced, considering they can save lives and all."

The man pursed his lips, picked up a whistle, and studied it. "Guess I could use one of these. Sure does do a lot of damage to your truck when you hit one of them deer. And them carcasses on the road, why that's a pitiful sight, ain't it?"

As I handed him his change, I smiled over at M.J.

We sat there in the shade of the tarp all morning, watching the crowd go by and talking to customers. Sales were good. I had to keep reaching down into my box and setting out a new supply of whistles.

The birdhouses went fast, too. M.J. chatted with the ladies and played with the little children who came by, while she sold one birdhouse right after another.

In between sales I couldn't help noticing all the groups of kids about my age who walked around talking and laughing. My eyes followed them until they disappeared down an aisle or until I had to wait on another customer.

As always, M.J. was watching *me.* "Before you go running off," she said, like she had read my mind, "pick out one of the barn-style birdhouses for yourself. You don't have one of them yet."

By now I knew better than to argue with M.J. So I searched through the boxes of birdhouses until I found the one I liked best. The bird hole was framed to look like a loft window. Below it, two swinging doors with crisscrossed wooden slats opened on hinges made of old leather. I set the birdhouse aside and then jumped up to go look around the fair.

Up and down the aisles, other local craftspeople sold everything from oil paintings, pottery, and handmade quilts to sheepskin jackets and beaded moccasins. Dealers from large companies sold farm machinery, hardware, and shiny new pickup trucks. The dealers stood in the shade of fancy tents, trying to talk farmers into making the big investment.

As I walked through the livestock area, I spotted

Dad down one of the aisles. He stood with Pansy, gently holding her lead. Next to him were a couple of teenage boys wearing gigantic cowboy hats.

I cringed and started to duck away. But then I turned back, just for a second, to take another look.

The boys seemed to be under Dad's spell. They stood perfectly still and listened as he explained away. "Alpacas are becoming more and more common in the United States, but about ninety-eight percent of the world's alpaca population still lives in Chile, Peru, and Bolivia."

I blinked hard. Amazing. These boys actually appeared to be interested.

I followed the next aisle into an enormous tent. Rows of animal pens lined the area, and fresh straw covered the ground. Cows of every color, pigs with whiskered snouts, chickens, ducks, geese, and lambs filled the tent.

Down the aisle in front of me, I saw somebody who looked familiar. It was Tim. I spun around and tried to get away unnoticed, but it was too late. I had been spotted.

"Hey, isn't that the Florida girl? Laney!" Tim called out after me.

I stopped and made myself turn around. He was standing with a boy and a girl who looked about my age and who wore the same countrified clothes as

Tim—boot-cut jeans, western shirts, and of course the ever-present cowboy hat. They walked up to me.

"We saw your alpaca," Tim said.

I searched his face. He was smiling, but in a friendly way. I let myself relax a bit.

"Pretty cool," one of the other kids was saying.

They thought the alpacas were cool?

"How many in your herd?" the girl asked.

"Twenty." I breathed out. "No, wait. Now we have twenty-one."

"One of them has already had a baby?" Tim asked.

I shrugged. "Beginner's luck, I guess."

Tim invited me to walk around with his friends, but I hesitated. Was I ready for this? Angela would never have had to ask herself that question. Where was Angela, anyway? I was surprised she hadn't glued herself to this little group already.

"Have you seen my sister?" I asked.

Tim nodded. "Shopping for horses."

I started walking with them down the aisles of the tent. We passed by a row of rabbit cages, and Tim pointed out the various breeds and categories for judging. Some of the rabbits were very small, while others were as big as one of M.J.'s tomcats. Some of them had little ears, and others had long, drooping ears.

Tim's friends dropped away when they saw somebody they knew grooming a steer for judging, but Tim continued to walk with me. He told me about all the animals that we passed. I had to admit it—he was pretty nice.

We worked our way through a crowd of people who had gathered around a big ring. Inside the ring, children and teenagers led white lambs with black faces into the open area. After they got their lambs in place, they adjusted the way the animals were standing. Tim explained that this was called "setting." The competitors had to make sure that the animals' feet were in the proper position or they'd lose points. Then the judge slowly walked around, behind, and between each of the lambs.

"This must be serious business," I whispered.

"You better believe it," Tim said under his breath. "There's a lot of money up for grabs." He leaned closer. "Pride, too."

After long minutes of looking and thinking, the judge finally took the microphone and announced the winners. Some people in the audience whooped and hollered as the names of the winners and their ranches were called.

"At the end of the fair, the animals are auctioned off," Tim explained as we walked away.

"Isn't it tough for those kids to have to give up their animals?"

Tim nodded. "Especially when they know what's going to happen."

I looked up. "What do you mean?"

With his hand, Tim sliced an imaginary knife across his neck.

His meaning slowly dawned on me. "You're kidding, right?"

"No, I'm not."

As we walked away, I thought about all of those animals I had just seen who were on their way to be slaughtered. At least my family didn't have to kill the alpacas. We only had to shear them.

Next, Tim and I entered the County Extension building, passing under a large, hand-painted banner that read, "Pig Roast and Dance Tonight." Inside the building we saw displays of every kind of crop imaginable—huge waxy squash, shiny tomatoes, zucchini, herbs, carrots, potatoes, beans. In another section we found contestants vying for ribbons in cake baking, sewing, photography, and other categories.

"What do you think of the fair?" Tim asked, suddenly turning to face me.

I tried to smile. I didn't want to say that it was just about the weirdest thing I had ever seen in my whole life. "It's different."

He took that as a compliment. "It's only going to

get better. Tonight we have a dance, and tomorrow there'll be tractor races and a rodeo."

"A rodeo?" I asked. I didn't even know those things still existed. "You mean, a *real* rodeo?"

Tim laughed. "Of course a real rodeo. This isn't a movie set, you know."

I felt my face flush. I was as ignorant about his world as he was about mine. I looked up and saw Tim's friends coming back.

"You know what? I'm supposed to be working." I pulled away. "I have to go."

"Hey, are you staying for the dance tonight?" Tim called after me.

I shook my head and continued walking backward. "I don't know how to dance to that kind of music." I couldn't imagine what I would do with myself at a country-western dance.

"You don't know the two-step?" He smiled.

"The what?" I blurted out. "No, I've never even heard of—" Suddenly I bumped into something. I turned around and saw a woman trying not to drop a cardboard tray full of drinks. Some of the soda was dripping down the sides of the tray. "Sorry," I mumbled. I had walked right into her.

"That's OK, sweetie," the woman said.

I could feel my face burning.

When I turned back, Tim was grinning in that

amused way, like the way he had on the day I'd met him. The other kids were smiling, too.

"I really have to go now," I stammered. I turned and rushed away as fast as I could.

"We'll stop by your booth later," Tim called out. "I hope you sell a lot of those deer whistles."

I couldn't tell if he was making fun of me or not.

I stayed at the booth for the rest of the day. When the crowd thinned out and the daylight dimmed, I looked over at M.J. She was still smiling, just as she had been doing all day long. But she looked tired. I saw lines in her face that I had never seen before.

I went searching for Dad to take us home. After I found him, we quickly packed up the car and helped M.J. into the front seat.

On the way home Dad glanced over his shoulder at me and asked, "You're planning to come back with me, aren't you? To go to the dance with Mom and Angela?"

"You should," M.J. announced. "It's always a lot of fun. Makes for interesting conversation for years to come."

"I don't think so," I muttered, looking out the window.

"Come on, Laney," Dad coaxed.

M.J. adopted her bossy tone. "Just drop me off and go back with your father."

I considered it for a minute. Staring out at the barren landscape, I thought of how nice all of the people seemed to be and how they'd shown interest in us and our alpacas. But then I thought about kids who raised lambs and went to rodeos and knew how to dance the two-step—kids I had nothing in common with. "No, I think I'll go home."

I saw Dad's shoulders fall and heard M.J. let out a big sigh.

[12]

the
storm

As soon as I got home, I went straight to my room and plopped down on my bed. I sat on the edge of it, staring out the window at the sky. The curtains on my window were flapping like sails in the wind.

I leaned forward. Something was happening. Huge, dark clouds were moving in and covering the last light on the horizon. Bursts of wind began to lash the stunted trees around our house. In the distance, bolts of lightning split through the sky, and thunder boomed. Each new lightning bolt came closer, and the thunder kept getting louder.

A storm, a big storm, was coming.

I watched leaves blow past my window. I caught

the scent in the wind, the smell of water and wet grass. I shut my window, lay back on the bed, and closed my eyes. My body ached with exhaustion, while my mind still reeled with new sights and sounds, faces and animals, smells and sensations.

I fell asleep.

I dreamed that I was walking on the beach when a hurricane suddenly came in from the ocean.

I woke up with my heart pounding. I lay there and studied the shadows on the ceiling, looking at the patterns and waiting for my heart to calm down. Suddenly a shiver jolted through me.

Something felt wrong. Very wrong. It was too quiet. Even through the rattle of thunder, I could hear an eerie silence. I didn't know what it was, but it gnawed at me. I sprang from the bed. Was it M.J.? She had looked so tired, and now she was all alone in that tiny trailer with no way to call if she needed help. I grabbed my denim jacket and ran outside.

I looked toward M.J.'s place, thrusting my arms into my jacket. Then out of the corner of my eye, I noticed the pasture.

Empty.

Only an hour before, when Dad had dropped me off, I had seen the alpacas standing in small groups around the food and water troughs. But now they were gone. Every single one of them.

Quickly I circled the pasture and found a portion of fence lying flat against the ground. In the dirt around it, I saw the alpacas' footprints. I turned and stared out in all directions. Storm clouds loomed overhead, and everything looked dark gray. I could see no sign of the herd.

I ran inside, grabbed my dad's binoculars, and came back out. Scanning the area, I saw nothing at first. Then, over toward the west, I saw some gray shapes that moved. I focused in and recognized the alpacas, grazing in the wash along the road.

I dropped the binoculars from my face. Of course that's where they would go. "They like to eat different kinds of vegetation," Dad had once said. And in the wash, all kinds of different grasses grew.

Another bolt of lightning cracked to the ground, and the first drop of rain hit me like a stone. I raced for the door. By the time I had reached the front porch, rain was pouring from the sky. Puddles formed all around me. As dry and hard as asphalt, the land couldn't absorb this much water at once.

Then, like the slap of a wave on sunburned skin, I remembered.

"Never stay in a wash when it rains," M.J. had told me.

I groped for the doorknob. I burst into the house and fell against the wall. The alpacas were in the wash, and it was raining. Raining hard.

The alpacas would drown.

I ran to the coat closet, threw off my denim jacket, found my dad's Gore-Tex rain jacket, and swung myself into it. I dashed to the garage and found Dad's best flashlight. Then I flew back outside.

My face got pelted with tiny white rocks coming out of the sky. They hopped across the hardened soil like little bouncing balls. Hail.

I clicked on the flashlight, looked toward the wash, and started out. I tried to run, but I slipped and fell, crunching down on the hail that now covered the ground. I pulled myself up and set out again.

Then I stopped.

What was I doing? My parents would never want me out in this storm. Not even to save the alpacas. They would want me to stay in the house until they returned. They would want me to try to phone someone at the dance and get a message to them. They wouldn't want me to do this.

But if I waited, it would be too late. All the alpacas would be dead. Even Pansy, who was safe for now at the fair, would eventually die without her companions. "They are very social animals. An alpaca separated from its herd slowly perishes from loneliness," Dad's book had said.

The hail changed to rain and back to hail again. I

stood and watched as my shoes began to sink into the slush.

No one would blame me for not going.

And isn't this just what I had predicted? Disaster? I could prove once and for all that my family was wrong, and our ranching days would immediately end. The alpacas were too costly to replace. I could be back in Florida before school started.

But as I stood there getting soaked by the storm, images started coming back to me. Even though I could see nothing except the beam of my flashlight, I could clearly picture the alpacas' faces, their shining dark eyes, and their cushy crimped coats. I could feel Ginger and Leotie eating out of my hand. I could hear the herd humming.

I shone the flashlight in front of me and started walking.

As I trudged forward, sliding and stumbling over the slick earth, a mixture of rain and hail continued to pound me. But I kept going, sweeping the beam before me. I could see no signs of the herd. I pushed on anyway, heading in the direction of the wash.

I didn't think the rain could hammer down any harder, but it did. My feet were soaked. Dad's jacket provided some protection for my body, but the hood was too big and kept blowing off my head. Soon my hair was drenched, the cold curls plastered against my face. Rain poured into my eyes. I pushed the hair off my face as my teeth began to chatter like a sack of bones.

Minutes later, I saw some scrub oak and patches of juniper. I exhaled deeply. The changed vegetation meant I had come near the wash.

Soon I stood on the rim looking down. No water rushed below me, at least for now. The dirt in the wash bed looked muddy from the rain, but the trench remained clear of any runoff. But where were the alpacas?

I swept the flashlight along the bed of the wash and found a few familiar toenail prints. They had been here. Did they cross over the wash and keep going? Or were they still somewhere in it, sampling and grazing?

I tramped along the rim, moving the beam along the creek bed. Every so often I saw more tracks and hoped that it meant I was heading in the right direction. I scrambled over juniper bushes and stepped over slick rocks. Rain ran down the sides of my face and dripped off my nose.

Finally my light landed on a fuzzy body. I swept the beam around and let out a sigh of unbelievable relief. There they were, the whole herd, munching on grasses and clover, not even slightly disturbed by the storm. These animals could survive in the Andes

Mountains, after all. The rain and hail of the prairie didn't bother them one bit.

I called out and clapped my hands. "Come on," I shouted. "Get out!"

The alpacas ignored me. I shone the flashlight right into their eyes and tried to startle them. "Move it!" I screamed.

They wouldn't budge. They were as content as could be, right where they were. I tried yelling and waving my arms, but nothing worked. The rain continued to pound me. I grew desperate. What should I do? What could I do?

The dirt in the wash bed was damp but remained firm. As the alpacas grazed, they didn't seem to be sinking or slipping. It was safe. I could go into the wash and drive them out.

I started down the bank. Halfway down, my shoes lost their grip in the mud and I slid the rest of the way. But I managed to stay standing. When I got to the bottom, I started clapping and screaming at the alpacas.

One by one, they started to clamber up the bank, with me yelling at them from behind.

At last, I thought, as the most stubborn ones finally scrambled out of the wash. Now they were all on higher ground and headed in the direction of the ranch. I grabbed a branch and pulled myself up the steep bank. I was shivering uncontrollably, but it didn't matter. I needed only to drive the herd back to the pasture, close them inside the barn for the night, take a long hot bath, and know that I had made the right decision.

I started walking. But I had taken only a few steps when I saw Ginger heading back in my direction.

It hit me. Leotie. Where was she?

I spun around and beamed the light into the wash. There was Leotie on the bottom, trying to climb out but struggling. Her slender legs dug at the slick earth as she groped for footing on the embankment.

"Come on, Leotie," I called. "Come on, you can do it."

I watched as the cria pawed and chopped at the mud. She started to climb, but as soon as she got a few feet up the bank, she slid back down.

I turned and shone the flashlight on the rest of the herd behind me. The alpacas were still heading toward the ranch, all of them except Ginger, who was waiting for her baby.

I scrambled back down the bank, swooped Leotie into my arms, and thrust her as high up on the bank as I could. Then I pushed her from behind. She stumbled but picked herself up, dug in her toenails, and went up and over the rim.

I let out a deep breath. It was over.

Then I heard it. A loud, rushing sound like the roar of big waves pounding the beach.

The water. The wall of water was coming.

I dropped the flashlight and groped for a branch. I wrapped my fingers around a stem of juniper and pulled. I got one foot on the side of the bank.

Then it slapped me, stole my legs, my breath, my world away. I was caught up in a rage of water. I hammered against it with my hands and legs and every ounce of strength in my body.

But the water swept me away.

[13]

a world
of water

Flowing, surging, churning water surrounded me. I tumbled around in a world of angry foam, and I was lost. No sense of surface or bottom, no sense of anything except fear. I clawed and battled against the current, my eyes frozen wide with terror. Before me I saw nothing but blackness and bubbles. I heard the muffled sounds of water whisking and coursing and rushing all around me.

My lungs would burst if I didn't find the surface soon. I kicked and pulled with all my might, but I only seemed to be taken away faster.

Maybe I should stop fighting. Maybe it would be easier to let it carry me away. It felt soothing in a strange way, being cocooned in a world of water.

No! I loved the water, but I didn't want to die in it. I groped and pushed and strained. My head burst above the surface. I gasped, breathing in deeply, sucking air into every inch of my lungs. Then I went under again.

Think, Laney. Don't panic.

My head broke through the surface once more. As soon as I had filled my lungs with air, though, I was blasted back under.

Think. Think. Concentrate on using your strength to stay near the surface.

For a few seconds, I let myself go with the flow so my muscles could rest. Then, following the bubbles to the surface, I swam up for air. I sucked in deep breaths before allowing myself to be swept away again. Down and up I went like this, going under with the current, then breaking through to the top.

Just when I thought my arms and legs would fall off from fatigue, the force of the current seemed to lessen. I was able to tread water and keep my head above the surface for a few seconds, maybe even a minute. Bobbing, I turned in all directions, trying to see something, anything. But the world around me looked black.

Try to get to the bank, the voice inside me screamed. I rolled onto my side and stroked the water. I knew

I needed to get out of the strong center current. I reached out as far as I could and pulled, over and over, but I didn't seem to be getting any closer.

My legs ached, and my body felt large and heavy. Suddenly I realized I still wore my dad's jacket. I tore my arms free of the sleeves and let it go. I kicked off my shoes. Without the coat and shoes, I could swim much better. I went under the surface and swam like a seal, stretching my body out and pushing across the current.

Time slowed, until finally the sound of the water no longer seemed to be coming from around me but from somewhere deep inside of me instead.

Merissa. Merissa of the sea, the words bubbled up. *You are stronger than this water.*

The tension in my muscles relaxed, and I felt a sense of calm flow through my bones.

I stroked hard. My fingers touched something. I tried to grasp it, but in an instant it was gone. I tried again. I reached and plunged sideways in the water, propelling myself toward the bank. *Please, please let me touch something again,* I prayed.

Finally my hand scraped against something stiff and sharp. It was a branch sticking sideways from the bank, just below the surface. I tried to grab it and missed, but I managed to hook my leg around it as the current carried me past. Then I wrapped my other leg around it, and with both legs coiled tightly around the branch like snakes, I held on with all the strength I could muster. I raised my head above the water and took a quick breath before dropping back under again. Then, pulling against the current with my arms, I dragged the rest of my body back toward the branch. I grabbed onto it with stiff, trembling fingers. I lifted my head out of the water.

I clung to that branch, my entire body shaking with fear, cold, and relief. As the current continued to push against me, I hung on, gulping in sweet air.

I don't know how long it took me, but slowly I inched my way along the branch toward the bank. I knew that one little slip, one moment of relaxation, could send me under again. At last I felt mud against my feet. I planted my toes in the side of the embankment and, still holding on to the branch with both hands, crept the rest of the way along it. Finally I was able to reach out and grab another branch, higher up.

I carefully searched for the next foothold and slowly hoisted myself up. Grunting and gasping, my hands clawing at the muddy earth, at last I crawled over the bank.

I fell onto my stomach. I lay facedown in the mud, choking and trembling and crying.

When I opened my eyes, a soft rain was falling

and gently pattering the mud beside my cheek. I rolled over and let the droplets sprinkle all over my face. I lay there and breathed deeply for a long time, unable to move. When my strength finally returned, I pushed myself to my feet and started walking.

I was chilled all the way down to my bones. My clothes clung to my goose-pimpled flesh, and I could no longer feel my fingers or toes, but I walked anyway. Soon I saw headlights, rows of headlights, sparkling in the distance.

A road. Everyone was coming home from the dance. I laughed out loud with relief. Nothing could have looked so beautiful to me at that moment as those ordinary lights showing me the way.

I forced myself to keep moving forward, putting one foot in front of the other, until at last I reached the road.

Everything that happened after that seemed unreal, like a deep dream.

The first car to come along stopped. The entire family sprang from the car as soon as they saw the condition that I was in. The children stared at my trembling body, and the mother tried to warm me with her hands. The father found a blanket in the trunk, wrapped me up, and set me down in the backseat. I remember nothing after that until I woke up the next morning, safe in my own bed.

When I opened my eyes, Mom was sitting on the edge of the bed while Dad stood with his hands hanging helplessly at his sides. My parents looked like they had received a shock more serious than if they'd actually been hit by lightning.

Mom picked up one of my hands and held it curled inside her own. The softest expression came over her face. She brought my hand slowly to her face and kissed it.

Then Dad spoke, delivering the inevitable scolding. "You shouldn't have gone after them."

I started to smile at the memory of the alpacas grazing happily in the wash. I smiled even bigger as I imagined their escape from the pasture. Had they schemed ahead of time to push down the fence and go on this little adventure? Or was it just a spur-of-the-moment field trip? I almost laughed out loud.

"Are you surprised?" I asked my parents.

Dad shook his head. "Surprised that you would go against your own feelings and risk yourself to save the alpacas?"

Mom said in her softest voice, "Not as surprised as you think."

[14]

the only
constant

I never knew how close I had come to drowning until I heard the locals retell the story about a hundred different ways.

All over two counties, M.J. reported to me, the scuttlebutt was spreading faster than a swarm of grasshoppers. Some people whispered I had clung to that branch for hours. Others said I had walked for miles, barefoot, lost in a fog. The old men who hung out in the barbershop swore the current ripped my shoes and even my socks right off my feet, and the owner of the general store told everyone that I needed seventy stitches from a plastic surgeon. The ladies at the quilting bee claimed that Dad's raincoat washed up somewhere in Kansas. The stories just kept getting better and better.

And almost every day, somebody drove out to our ranch to look at the alpacas. I could see people glancing at me out of the corner of their eyes while they made conversation with my parents.

Mom and Dad loved the opportunity to tell everyone about the alpacas. And Angela, who was a little jealous at first of all the attention I was getting, enjoyed glomming on to all our new visitors, thrilled at the chance to turn on her charms.

When families with children came, of course, the kids cooed over Leotie and wanted to pet her. But I made everyone stay away from Leotie. Ever since the storm she had become skittish, fearful of everything and everybody. If she didn't glue herself to Ginger's leg, she hid herself within the safety of the herd.

Even Mom and Angela couldn't get near Leotie. Often they tried to approach after the visitors had left, but as soon as she caught their scent, she trotted away and hid herself again.

Her only human contact was when she let me feed her through the gate. Every day I found a clump of green grass for her. But if I tried to enter the pasture, she bolted away. So I stayed on the other side of the gate.

In the meantime, we had work to do. Summer

was nearly over and, in addition to all of our other chores, Angela and I had to get ready for school. We filled out our papers at the registrar's office. At the general store, we bought school supplies and new backpacks. And for school clothes, we headed over to Kmart, where Mom, Angela, and I spent an entire day darting in and out of the dressing rooms. Angela picked out lacy tees and skirts with matching tights, while I chose bulky sweatshirts and jeans.

One day, when we were in the shoe department, I was trying on a new pair of running shoes and suddenly felt someone's eyes resting on me. I glanced down the aisle and saw Tim standing there with the guy I had met at the fair.

This time I didn't duck away. I looked right at them and waved. They smiled and walked up to me.

"Hi," I said.

"Hey, Florida. How does it feel to be the talk of the county?" Tim joked.

I grinned. "Still haven't gotten my dad's raincoat back from Kansas."

They laughed.

"So, are you OK?" Tim finally asked.

I shrugged. "I came out in one piece."

Tim stuck his hands into his pockets and smiled. "Even the high school kids will want to know how you managed to do that."

But I didn't care about impressing high school kids. I thought about how people were admiring me for only part of what I had done. Rescuing the alpacas was a pretty big deal, but the thing I felt really proud of was the thing I had planned and worked hard for. The thing that eventually might save the lives of a lot more animals than I did the night of the storm. On the way back from Kmart, I noticed it for the first time—a few cars and trucks with deer whistles mounted on their front bumpers.

It wasn't a lot, but it was a good start.

That evening I stayed in my room, staring out the window just as I had done on our first day here. I turned from the window and stared at all the boxes still lined up against the walls.

The time had come.

I ripped off the packing tape and dug inside the first box. I unloaded all of my books and magazines and lined them up on the bookcase. I opened another box and pulled out the stuffed animals I had saved from when I was little, and I set them up at the foot of my bed. I assembled and connected my stereo system and picked out a CD to play. I arranged my framed photos and glass figurines on my desk. I worked until I had emptied all of the boxes. All except for one.

The box marked *Shells*.

I let my eyes rest on it for a few minutes. Then I knelt down and carefully opened the flaps.

I unrolled the bubble wrap and placed each shell on the windowsill. First my bright orange sea star, then spider fingers of red coral and ovals of shiny, pearl-like abalone. I unwrapped my sand dollar, rare because it had no chips or cracks. I freed my striped nautilus shell from its wrapping and wiped off the dust before placing it next to the others.

Then I looked up at M.J.'s birdhouse. Since the storm, M.J. had been smiling at me in the same way she smiled at one of her finished pieces. "It was the solid ground that saved you, you know," she'd say with one of her winks.

And now my shells sat overlooking the prairie, a land that was once covered by a shallow sea. Maybe they weren't so far from home after all.

The first time I had gazed out the window and let myself look at the land, really study it, I had thought I was staring into nowhere. But now I was learning to notice things, like the way the colors of the earth changed as the sun sank low in the sky and the way the scent of sage got stronger after a rain. Learning that hard earth underfoot could sometimes be what I wanted, and needed, most of all.

★

The next morning I awoke while the light was still dim. I finished my chores quickly so I would have time to run over to M.J.'s and tell her about the deer whistles I had seen on the way back from Kmart. Before I left, however, I checked the pasture and counted all the alpacas. Then I looked around for a special treat for Leotie.

While I fed her through the gate, I remembered swooping her up in the wash. I remembered the way she had felt in my arms, all warm and slippery, and how tiny she had seemed. How the earthy smell of her was even stronger when her wool was wet.

I stood up and looked around. Since the storm, several more rains had fallen, and the prairie had greened up. Emerald-colored patches of clover and thick blades of grass dotted the brown dirt every-where. I bent down and pulled up an especially rich-looking clump of grass.

Then I slipped inside the gate. Holding out my hand, I crouched down and waited for Leotie to come to me. I waited until my legs ached to stretch out again. Leotie watched me from a few yards away, with those big black eyes of hers. I looked right back, pleading with her to stop being scared.

She took one step forward. Then she hesitated. She pawed at the dirt with one foot and waited for what seemed like forever. Then finally she started coming forward, her head slightly tilted to one side. When she reached me, she stopped, sniffed the ends of my fingers, took a mouthful of grass from my opened palm, and let me lay my other hand on her withers.

"Hello, Leotie," I said, stroking her spine.

She cleaned every blade of grass from my hand, even the tiny pieces that had slipped between my fingers. Then she turned her nose upward and sniffed all the way up my arms to my face. I closed my eyes and felt her warm breath.

One of M.J.'s favorite quotations popped into my head. *Nothing endures but change,* from Heracleitus, another Greek philosopher. "It's the only thing we can really count on," M.J. had said.

I stood up and stretched. An image of Florida came to me. But it wasn't of the beach, and not of the ocean, either. Instead it was of being in the old Subaru wagon, riding down the winding roads of the Everglades.

I am in the backseat, smiling. Up ahead I can see a big curve in the road, veering away out of sight. Dad is driving fast, and it feels as if the car is gripping the road with only two tires instead of all four. We don't have a clue what we'll find around the bend.

And still, I am smiling.

Ann Howard Creel

Then

Now

As a girl growing up in Texas, Ann Howard Creel spent many weekends on the beach at Galveston Island. But after moving to Denver, Colorado, where she still lives today, she came to love the nearby mountains as much as the ocean of her youth. She is married and has three sons, two dogs, and one cat.